THE GIRL WHO BROUGHT DARKNESS

BOOKS OF DARKNESS 2

BLAZEJ DZIKOWSKI

Editing by Lee at Ocean's Edge Editing

First Edition

ISBN 978-83-942182-2-5

www.blazejdzikowski.com

CONTENTS

TO KILL A HOME

GABRIEL STOPPED his bike in the courtyard of their apartment building. The slab of black wall towered above him against the dark navy sky, dotted here and there with yellow lights of the windows where people worked all night, or a blinking silver glow where they watched late-night TV. A wave of memories hit him like a punch straight in the heart.

"I suppose your old home ranks pretty high on the list if someone is searching for you," said Maurice, the demon of his leather wristband.

Gabriel didn't answer. He chained his bike to the stand, crossed the courtyard to the entrance, and punched in the code. The door buzzed, he opened it, and entered the dark hallway.

He saw envelopes sticking out of the slot in their full post-box, but he didn't make a move to take any. Mail was for people living on the bright side of reality.

He turned back to the entrance to the house and said, "Come out."

The demon of the door was a sleepy, ill-tempered guy in janitor clothes.

"I am the demon of the door to poor men's house. Many times I've been kicked or spat at, or hit with a body thrown with violence against me, and many tired hands opened me while trying to hold heavy bags at the same time! I know you, dark teenage boy. You lived here with your brother, but then you were gone. Policemen took you away."

"Stop talking already," murmured Gabriel, and looked around uncomfortably, afraid that a neighbor might see him. He pulled his hood lower over his face.

"I just want you to know I'm on your side!" said the Door. "You're not the first resident to be led outside by cops, and I always open to them with the highest degree of reluctance. I wouldn't do that at all, if only opening and closing wasn't my duty and my fate."

"That's good to hear," Gabriel said. "Are there any strangers in the building right now?"

"One granny came with a visit to the granny who always wears purple."

"You mean Mrs. Ludmila. Anyone else?"

"Three couples, men and women, with flowers and bottles, alcohol I presume. They smelled of perfume and had their hair nicely done."

"Must be a party. No strange men who don't live here?"

"Negative. But tell me, young man who lived here for so long, how come you see me and talk to me when I remained invisible to you before?"

Gabriel ignored this question.

"I'm back," he said to the demon, and made the Sign of the Covenant. "When a stranger comes by and tries to enter, don't open without my approval. Tell the stairs. They will tell the elevators. They will tell the hallway, and it will tell my apartment, who will let me know. Is it understood?"

"Absolutely, Ombudsman! If I may say ... I had no idea someone so important lived in my building..."

Gabriel left the demon of the door and went to the elevators. It was the first time he'd come back since the policemen and Agent Delancey had taken him away after his mother's death.

THE DOOR to their apartment was secured with paper seals. *These premises have been sealed by the Los Maines police dept. pursuant to...* etc. He touched one of them.

"Open up," he said to the door.

The door creaked; he heard the lock open and the door pulled apart, tearing off the seals.

"Stop," Maurice said, looking into the apartment. "Gabriel. Don't go in there."

But Gabriel stepped inside, his heart beating fast, and he couldn't understand what he saw. In the faint light coming from the hallway, he saw every object in their apartment, the floor, the walls, the clothes rack, even the lamp and the ceiling—everything looked like it was made of porous, black lava, reminding him of dry pumice stone. He took more careful steps, each of them stirring up clouds of black soot. He understood the apartment and everything in it was dead.

"What is it?" he whispered to Maurice. "Have you ever seen anything like this?"

Maurice shook his head, nervously.

"It looks like ... burned or something," Gabriel said.

The strange floor creaking under his footsteps, he went deeper into the apartment. It was like walking in an echoey underground chamber, or a cave. The black dust swirled in the air.

"What happened here?" Gabriel whispered, but there was nobody to answer him. "What terrible smell..."

The whole place smelled of old, burned hair. The smell reminded him of the time he escaped the burning prison that had been struck by the fallen airplane, but in here everything was dark and silent.

He entered his mother's room, similarly transformed. The lights through the windows cast dim reflections on the pumice interiors. Gabriel cleared his constricted throat and touched the rough surface of the wardrobe where his mother kept her clothes.

"Come out," he said with difficulty, trying to invoke the demon.

"It's dead," Maurice said. "Every demon in this place has been killed. This place is death."

Gabriel went through the rooms, looking for anything that had remained intact.

"Maybe it's even better that way," he said. "I was a fool for coming here. I couldn't bear staying here anyhow, after all that happened."

Gabriel looked around the dark, foreboding space filled with petrified fossils of furniture he'd known since the day he was born. He felt like crying. Everything had been taken away from him.

He went back to the hallway and called out the demons of the police seals. They were scared and overzealous, like low-level corporate workers. They bowed a lot.

"We are put on doors to important areas, where secrets abide!" they exclaimed, speaking over each other. "We make sure nobody enters to discover that which must remain hidden! Until the official masters come and remove us! Yes, but no sooner than they log down the act of our breaking in their important books! That's right and correct!"

"Interesting," Gabriel said. "And who put you on this door?"

"The policemen did," came the answer. "They said a terrible crime was committed in this apartment and it needed to remain locked until the proceedings end. Yes! And until the state decides what happens with the property. That's right! That's correct!"

Gabriel was silent for a second after the Seals mentioned the crime. They meant him killing his mother, when he thought she was Ricko Boleani, the sadistic, face-changing kidnapper.

"And when the police put you on this door, the apartment was already like that? Dead?"

The Seals looked at each other. It was apparent they didn't know what he was talking about.

"Or did you open for someone? And then close again, as if nothing had happened?"

"The killers, they didn't come through the door," said a sad, female voice.

"Who's that?" He turned his head in alarm.

"Welcome back, Gabriel."

Next to him there stood a dejected, middle-aged woman, with a weary face of a bluish tint like all demons. Wearing a simple dress and her hair long, she looked at Gabriel and smiled softly and he felt as if he knew her from somewhere. She felt familiar, almost mother-like.

"I am the door to your apartment," she said. "I've known you since you were so little. You and Matt. Always slamming me so hard, despite your mother's admonitions. I kept guard to your little world, protecting your safe sleep for years. And it wasn't through me that those who killed your rooms entered."

"How did they enter, then?"

The Door lowered her stare and shrugged.

"I just heard ... terrible screams. All demons of your apartment screamed in agony. And my inward eyes saw the walls, the floors, the beds and chairs and pictures turn to black, dead stone. And I heard footsteps behind the walls. Two light-footed men. Making inhuman sounds. Like ... snorting, and laughing, and squealing. All happy, like at a stag party..."

"When was it?"

"It was last night."

"Did you see them?"

"Just heard."

Gabriel went back into the apartment, straight to the living room. The door to the balcony hung there all broken in its hinges.

He went out to the balcony, eleven floors above the dark streets of the poor district, next to the identical high-rise tenements. Cold wind was blowing. Leaning against the rail, he looked down to the empty courtyard far below, flooded with a milky glow from streetlights. Then he raised his hands to look at them; they were covered with dark film from the rail—the balcony was dead too.

His family apartment was like a decaying hole in the body of the building.

"Did they fly in here?" Maurice said in wonder. "How else?"

Gabriel just looked at him without answering, clenched his jaw and made a wide gesture with his hand.

"House!" he said. "Come out!"

A translucent colossus, as tall as their high-rise, appeared in the air, crouching next to them. His naked body was covered with pronounced muscles, like chiseled from stone. He moved his majestic face close to the balcony, obscuring the whole view, and squinted his huge eyes with irises as big as Gabriel. The colossus kept silent, just staring at the little boy on the high balcony.

"I am a Seer and an Ombudsman," Gabriel called to him. "I lived here, but my living place was destroyed. I want to know who did it."

It took the Building several good seconds before he answered in low, guttural tones.

"I am your house. Many families and many single people live inside of me, and I recognize you as well, tenant," the giant spoke. "I've seen people conceived, people born, and people die, murders and suicides, joys of a little child and anguish of lonely nights, when desperate people cry and shake their fists at the ceiling above them."

"Fascinating," Maurice whispered to Gabriel, rolling his eyes. "Does everyone here have to be so long-winded?"

But the boy gestured at him to be quiet.

"People are always afraid of the streets at night," the Building continued. "You know that, little human? While the worst things, the quiet horrors, always happen at home. We are like traps."

"He can really sell himself," commented Maurice, who apparently felt nervous faced with the humungous demon. "Should work as a real estate agent."

"Whatever you think, House," Gabriel answered the demon in a loud voice so his words could reach the giant ears, "But I was happy when I lived here, inside your walls, with my mother and brother. We had little, but we had each other. Terrible things happened and our world got shattered to pieces. And now even my apartment is destroyed. Do you know who did that?"

The Building was silent for a while, as if meditating on the question. And then, he hissed: "Men in white. Beautiful like angels. How they arrived, I didn't see."

"Okay," Gabriel exchanged looks with Maurice. The demon of the playground looked surprised. "And how did they get in?"

"They scaled my walls. They dashed up on all fours. Like quick little lizards."

Gabriel looked at Maurice with fear.

"Doesn't sound like the government people at the orphanage," he said. "More Ombudsmen? But I can't run on walls..."

"I don't think—" Maurice started to argue, but the Building interrupted him.

"Now, I want to sleep," he said. "Poor people have to get up at dawn and go to their jobs in the factory, in the port, in the warehouses. We need sleep."

Gabriel nodded in agreement.

The demon of his apartment house closed his giant eyelids and dissolved in the night air.

GABRIEL SAT on a bench in the courtyard. He didn't know what time it was. Maybe around 3 a.m.? Maurice stood next to him. They stared at the high-rise with its windows going dark one by one as the last tenants went to sleep.

"Men in white, beautiful like angels," Gabriel repeated what the Building told him. "Able to scale walls like lizards. Does that mean anything to you?"

Maurice hesitated. "Don't know about beautiful. But I heard about Princes. I thought it was just a stupid legend…"

"Princes? Of what?"

Maurice sighed and pushed his shabby hat to the back of his head.

"I don't know of what. That's what they're called. Princes. Demon-killers. And they can kill demons, as part of the covenant between us and men. To punish us, or to ensure men's control over their creation."

"And then, what happens with the totem?"

"It dies along with the demon. Like what happened with your home."

"Maybe they want to make me a Prince, too," he finally said.

"Yes, and this is why they destroyed your home," Maurice answered. "As an invitation to Princehood."

Gabriel gave him a bitter smile. Then, he rubbed his eyes.

"I'm so tired. I have to find a place to rest. Maybe I'll try Agent Delancey."

"I don't know about him."

"Why? He helped me find Matt."

"That was his job, wasn't it? He works for the government to find wanted people," answered Maurice, looking at Gabriel with his shiny, lava-like eyes. "And currently … one of them is you."

· · ·

THERE WAS a closed drugstore at the corner. The owner had had enough of being robbed at gunpoint every other night and shut the shop down. Now the space stood empty, advertising its "for rent" status on the white-painted windows. Gabriel told the alarm to be quiet and for the lock to open. The inside was empty, just some overturned, broken shelves, torn pieces of plastic sheeting, and smashed cardboard boxes. He told the door to lock behind him and not let in anyone else.

He folded several cardboard boxes into a simulacrum of a mattress and lay down. He pulled up his knees up to his chest to keep himself warm, pulled his hood over his face and closed his eyes. That was his first night outside the orphanage.

2

______

THEY ENTER

Boom! And the wail of sirens.

Andrea sat up in her bed, breathing heavily, her skin glistening with sweat.

It was the middle of the night and the whole house resounded with alarms. She heard her father running up the stairs.

"Andrea? Andrea!" He dashed into her bedroom and turned on the light. She squinted; her eyes hurt.

"What happened?" she asked.

He didn't answer straight away. He just stood there in his satin pajamas, trying to gather his thoughts, breathing quickly, and finally said:

"Lock the door. Don't come out!"

She didn't listen. She followed him into the hallway and watched him go into his office. Pele, their basset hound, stood on his short legs at the top of their wide, marble staircase and looked down to the first floor as if paralyzed with whatever he sensed there.

"Police?" she heard her father say on his phone. "Willows Avenue, one hundred and ten. I think there's an intruder in our house."

She felt a cold shiver. Her father came out of his office with a gun in his hand.

"Dad..." she whispered, "what's going on?"

He put his finger over his lips to tell her to be quiet. With the gun in his trembling hand, he began to sneak down the stairs. She followed him.

The first floor below them was completely dark.

"Who's there?" he called into the darkness.

The sirens of their alarm system suddenly went quiet, as if in an answer to his question.

They stood on the stairs. Andrea felt the wind on her face and she heard the sounds of the outside: the rustling of branches, droning cicadas, the cry of a night bird. She realized that the front door was open.

"I have a gun!" her father said.

Another cry from the bird in the yard sounded like a mockery of his threat.

Her father clenched his jaw and carefully went down to the last stair. He reached out, found the switch, and turned on the light.

"Oh, shit..." he whispered.

Holding her breath, Andrea tiptoed down to him and looked over his shoulder.

Their front door lay on the floor. Wind fell through the empty doorframe. What kind of force could rip the huge oak door off its hinges and iron lock pins?

"Dad..." Andrea whispered.

Her father looked around, aiming his gun into the corners. There was no one in the living room. A few dark branches scratched at their French doors to the terrace. Everything looked just as they had left it last night. The clock on the wall read three in the morning.

"I'll check the other rooms," he whispered to her.

"No, please," she whispered back, "Let's wait here."

"For what?"

"What are you going to do if someone's there?"

"Don't worry."

Andrea watched her father sneak through the living room and enter the kitchen. Her heart pounded so strongly she could feel it in her chest. She waited in fear for his scream but heard only his careful footsteps. The door to the guest room squeaked —he was now checking there.

Suddenly she gasped, hearing footsteps coming from outside. Someone approached their front door, more than one person. A stern, male voice said:

"Hello?"

Andrea found that she could not respond. She could only look on as the footsteps approached the front door, and someone came inside...

Two men—with shaved heads and black uniforms. One held a gun, the other a flashlight. The one with the flashlight flinched when he noticed Andrea in the corner of his eye. He screamed and pointed the blinding light at her. She squinted. The other aimed his gun at her.

"Don't move! Security!" he yelled.

Of course: the burglar alarm system sent an alert to their security company. They arrived very quickly, you had to give them that.

"Good evening," Andrea's father said, coming into the living room.

"Are you the owner of the house?" the security guard asked.

"Yes, Francis Bay. Someone broke down our door."

"We need to ask you for the code word."

"Yes, of course. Uh ... I'm not sure I remember it right, it's been so long since we set it up ... five years. It's either 'light' or 'bright.' Am I correct?"

The two guys looked at each other, then one of them sighed and nodded.

"Okay, we're going to accept that, sir. The word is 'brightness.' Did you check the house?"

"I didn't find anyone." Her father shook his head. "But I didn't have time to look everywhere. And then there's the yard..."

"We'll do that, don't worry. Please stay here."

Andrea's dad made a face at her, meaning: "See? It's all right."

He sat down next to her on the stairs and placed the gun in his lap. She stared at the deadly device. It was black and shiny.

They waited while the two security guards went from room to room.

"Aren't you cold?" asked Father.

She shook her head. Then she remembered something and asked him: "How did they get in?"

"What?"

"The security people."

"Oh. The company has the remote for our gate. When they get an alarm, they grab the remote, jump in their car, and drive off."

She nodded and thought some more.

"What happened to our door?" she asked.

"I have no idea, kid. It's so weird."

They heard the wail of a police siren.

One officer's name was Lasalle; his partner mumbled his name too quietly to understand. They talked with the security guards, the two teams treating each other with obvious hostility, and together they searched the grounds and every room of the house.

Francis and Andrea sat at the kitchen island. He made coffee for everyone. Andrea sipped her coffee and grimaced. It tasted very bitter to her.

"What kind of blend is it?" she asked her father.

"The usual. Valentino's. Why?"

"Tastes funny."

She poured in two spoonfuls of sugar. That killed the strange taste somewhat.

Lasalle walked in, and Andrea felt his eyes on her body. She adjusted herself. She'd forgotten they were still in their pajamas, sitting among the uniformed men. But her father didn't seem to mind. He had a very relaxed attitude towards people in the service industry.

"We've checked everything," Lasalle said.

"Yeah?" Francis put down his coffee cup and stood up.

"We didn't find anyone."

"Okay?"

"But we noticed those..." The policeman pointed to a surveillance camera in the corner of the room. "And one on the front porch."

"Yeah, those came with the house ... but I never actually turned them on. I didn't see any reason for it in this neighborhood."

"There you have it," Lasalle said. "I suggest you leave them on."

"Okay. But have you determined what happened here?"

"That's a good question, sir. I have a theory."

"Well, my door got ripped off its hinges. I think we really need a good theory here."

"There's no sign of damage, no scratches on the door surface that would come from a battering ram or anything like that. A strong force must have been applied to the door and the hinges gave way."

"But what kind of force? No one could just kick it and boom, no door. Maybe a motorcycle or something?"

"Like I said, no sign of impact. But I've heard of a weather phenomenon And with the weather going apeshit as it is, I think that's what we're dealing with here."

"Weather?"

"Yeah, like, a mini-tornado."

"Are you making fun of me?"

"A very localized tornado. A powerful gust of wind that did your door in. Don't believe wind can do that? In Florida, it lifts entire houses into the air. Nature is powerful, sir."

"But ... just the door? The windows are whole and intact, and wouldn't there be like, branches torn off the trees in the back yard, and so on?"

Officer Lasalle just stood there, visibly displeased with Andrea's father's skepticism.

"That's what we've got," he said finally. "If you kept your security camera on, we would have the definite answer. As it is, we're wrapping up."

The cops left. Then the security guards came into the kitchen, said some words critical of the police's work, and asked if Francis wanted them to do anything else.

"Do you have any ideas how anyone could do this?" asked Francis.

"Aside from the broken door, there's no sign of forcible entry," the security guard said. "No scratches from a crowbar or the like. Let me tell you how I see it."

"Okay."

"Imagine I'm this huge guy. Like, three hundred pounds. A brawler, down on his luck. Maybe my girl cheated on me or I got the boot at work. So I go into town for the night, I get drunk, or high, I'm out of my mind, you see? And on the way home I see your house. A beautiful house. I get really angry. 'I'll show those dirty exploiters,' I think."

"Who?"

"Rich people. So I climb over the gate, and I run like crazy, and ram into your door. I'm heavy like a bear and run real fast. Bam! Your door is busted. But then the alarm goes off. I get scared and get the heck out of here, as fast as I can."

There was silence.

"That's the way I see it," said the security guard, and his friend nodded.

"Do you think," Francis said, "that it might have been a mini-tornado after all?"

"What?"

Francis sighed.

"Okay, thank you, gentlemen. That'll be all."

The security guards grabbed some more coffee, and cinnamon buns from yesterday, and left.

Francis turned to Andrea. "I asked Claudine to come today. We're going to feel better with her around. I was supposed to go to work this morning, but as it is, I'll go in the afternoon..."

"On Sunday?"

"Yeah, we're having this super important merger. But for now, let me find a company that's open today to fix our door. Try and get some rest, kid."

$$3$$

VOICES IN THE LEAVES

LATER, her father made another round of the yard and the house. He made sure to open every cupboard and look behind every curtain. There was no doubt about it: they were the only people in the house at Willow Avenue 110.

Claudine arrived. The three of them carried the heavy door outside. Claudine stroked Andrea's hair, kissed her on the forehead and called her a poor *niña*. She always seemed to forget Andrea was no longer a child. She would sometimes bring her lollipops or cut the meat on her plate.

Then came the construction workers and the house vibrated with Pele's angry barking and their roaring drills as they installed new hinges and locks.

Meanwhile, her father downloaded the surveillance app on his phone and managed to turn on the cameras.

He showed Andrea the video stream on his phone. They could switch cameras by swiping across the screen. There were two in the hallways of each floor, one showing the backyard, one for the front porch, and one at the gate.

Then Andrea remembered the test for her literature class. She was supposed to finish reading *One Hundred Years of Solitude*, but with the noise the workers made, she moved to the back yard, where there was some quiet and a hammock in the shade. She took a couple of cushions with her and a gourd of maté that Claudine prepared.

Andrea lay down on the hammock and covered herself with a blanket.

She stared at the book in her hands and thought of Gabriel West, the mysterious boy from school. She found herself thinking about him more and more often. She was puzzled by him. He was touched by fate. This tragedy with the disappearance of his brother and the murder of his mother, and having to live in an institution, made Gabriel seem so much more mature than his peers. There was darkness in his face. Sometimes she toyed with the idea that she was in love with him. She tried to spend more time with him at school, but he always went quiet when they were together. And when she tried to talk to him, he never carried on the conversation, answering curtly and not looking her in the eye. She was afraid that he thought she was stupid and simple-minded, that she led a gaudy, problem-free life.

Saddened by these thoughts, she opened the book and wanted to read, but after only one page she found herself too tired to continue. Sleepiness overcame her often the last few days. Reality blurred and she felt like when her friend Mila brought Xanax pills to school that she'd stolen from her mother.

The wind touched her. She could feel each of its separate breaths. She could feel the patches of warmth where the sunlight falling through the foliage above touched her skin. She propped her head on the pillow and closed her eyes. Her breathing slowed.

Andrea, Andrea, a voice whispered. The wind stroked her cheeks.

She sighed. In a half-dream, behind her closed eyes, she saw herself walking through the grass toward the bushes in the back, toward the whirlpool of darkness in their very heart, whispering and calling her.

"Andrea?"

She opened her eyes. Her father stood in the terrace door, in his well-pressed shirt and suit.

"I'm going to work. Claudine will take care of the workers."

It took her a while to understand what he said. Lately she kept having this condition where she couldn't grasp the meaning of words. She could see people moving their mouths, and she could hear the sounds coming from their throats, but the sensations overwhelmed her and she couldn't follow. So she just nodded and turned to her side.

And suddenly it was evening. She saw it was getting dark, and her father stood next to the hammock, saying something with concern in his voice.

"You slept here all day?"

Andrea noticed that Claudine had covered her with a blanket while she slept.

She tried to remember anything of the past day, but she couldn't. She just stared at him, blinking her eyes, trying to understand what he wanted.

And then she smelled it. A heavy, earthy smell emanating from the paper bag in his hand.

"I need to lie down," she said, getting out of the hammock and walking toward the house.

He grabbed her arm.

"What's wrong? Are you sick?" He touched her forehead with his hand. "You don't have a fever..."

His hand was warm, and Andrea could feel a pulse ticking away in a vein hidden in his soft palm. She moved her head away.

"I just want to sleep," she said.

"It's not even night yet, and you've slept all day! Aren't you going to eat dinner? I brought chili." He showed her the paper bag.

She sat at the kitchen table and watched her father move the food out of the cardboard boxes onto the plates. He took off his jacket and pulled up the sleeves of his white shirt.

"I had some people from the security company stay in a van out on the street for the night," he said, setting the plate beside her.

She got her portion of red, grainy matter, with a tortilla on the side. She stared at the perfectly round tortilla. It reminded her of a full moon. It hypnotized her.

"Hello?" Francis asked, and waved his hand in front of Andrea's eyes. "Is there anybody in there?"

There was no answer. He put his hand on hers. "Andrea?"

"Leave me alone!" she screamed at him, and took her hand away. She got up and ran upstairs to her room. She jumped onto her bed without even bothering to close the door. She could hear her father making a call downstairs.

"Hi, Bob ... it's Francis. My daughter is acting strange and I wanted to get an expert opinion..."

She heard him sigh and scratch his head, and she realized she shouldn't be able to hear all this from such a distance. Her senses were sharpened. She smelled the meat and suddenly felt a great hunger.

She ran back downstairs, very quietly. Her father was in his room and couldn't hear her. She ran into the kitchen and grabbed fistfuls of chili and stuck it into her mouth, chewing and swallowing with immense hunger, like an animal. With the hot food in her belly she felt better. She returned to her bedroom, lay down, and closed her eyes. Her bed seemed to sway. And she fell into a deep dream.

It was a dream of old, ancient days before time, a dream that smelled of earth and blood, full of battle cries. She dreamed of hallowed places in the heart of a forest, of fear and whispers among the roots. Then she dreamed a night, with a fat, red moon. A night panting with animal desire, under shivering blue leaves, in a forsaken paradise. A strange bird sang among the trees. It sounded unearthly, like a human voice coming through the throat of a nightingale.

She woke up with a scream. And when she ran out of air, she took a deep breath, up to the brim of her lungs, and started to scream again.

Her father ran into her bedroom and shook her by the shoulders.

"What's going on?" he cried in desperation.

She stared at him with fear and pleading.

"I had a bad dream," she said finally.

FRANCIS TOOK her to his bedroom. It was 4 a.m. She lay on his bed and watched him sitting by his desk, going over reports on his iPad. He didn't even try to go back to sleep. It was starting to get light outside.

"Daddy?" she said suddenly.

"Yes?" he turned to her.

"I'm afraid of what's happening to me," she whispered.

"But ... what is happening to you?" He sat down beside her with concern on his face.

"I'm getting very strange thoughts ... which I can't even put into words," she whispered. "I feel as if I was falling into some kind of darkness."

He took her in his arms. It was the first time they'd hugged maybe in ten years. She hadn't needed any of his affection before. Or maybe that was her way of punishing him for her mom going away.

"It's been a very strange weekend," he whispered into her hair. "But we're going to have a very ordinary week. Yes, baby?"

Andrea nodded. She tried to believe that.

•　•　•

MONDAY STARTED like every other Monday. She came downstairs to the breakfast Claudine had prepared. Pancakes with jam for her. For Francis, omelet and cured turkey—he tried to eat low-carb.

"I think you should stay home with Claudine today," he said, carefully. "Try to get some more rest. I'll call your school. And when I get back, we'll drive over to Uncle Bob's."

"Okay, Dad," she said.

She went out to the back yard with her blanket and lay down in the hammock again.

FRANCIS DROVE through the congested streets to the Los Maines' business district, where his company, Maxravel Speditions, had its home among the forest of skyscrapers.

He walked down the carpeted hallways, greeted respectfully by other employees, until he arrived at his office.

"Hello, Susa," he said to his personal assistant.

"Good day, Director," she answered, looking up from her monitor. "Alek needs to see you ASAP."

"The merger?"

"Seems so."

Francis sighed, left his briefcase in his room, and went to the restroom.

At times as hectic as they were now, the moments he spent in the humming silence of the company restroom, standing over the urinal and letting his stare idle on the light above, were the only times he felt he could rest. He thought about the visits there as his only vacation.

He set his phone to "don't disturb" and entered Alek's office.

They talked for exactly an hour. Alek had a habit of operating in strict time segments, dividing his life into fifteen-minute chunks. Francis got four of them that morning.

As Francis left the CEO's office, he checked his phone and saw he had one unanswered call from Andrea and a recorded message on his voicemail.

On his way back to his office, he listened to it. It was just a second or so long—just her single breath, a rustle, and the recording cut.

Francis stopped in the corridor, frowned, and called Andrea. She didn't pick up the phone. Then he called Claudine. No answer.

He walked over to the reception area and sat down in a recliner. His heart was beating fast. He turned on the surveillance app.

At first he thought something had broken and he chortled with disbelief. There was the ocean on the screen, stretching out to the horizon: waves moving calmly in their eternal ebb and flow, and a fragment of a gray, sharp-edged rock in the lower right corner of the screen. It was supposed to be the feed from the front porch. But then he switched to the living room camera and saw only the ocean from a slightly different angle. Kitchen camera. First floor. Back yard. All cameras showed only the ocean and the fragment of a rock hanging above the waves.

His throat went dry. His heart raced. He tried calling Andrea again. She didn't pick up.

Without speaking to anyone, he took the elevator down to the underground garage, got into his SUV, and drove home as fast as he could.

HE RAN into the living room and heard the loud hum of a vacuum cleaner. When Claudine saw him, she turned it off and looked at him with surprise.

"Is there something wrong?" she asked.

"Where's Andrea?" he snapped.

"In the back yard ... reading..."

He stormed out the terrace door. He saw the hammock was empty. He walked over to it. There was the book she was reading on the cushion, and a crumpled blanket.

"Andrea!" he yelled.

"I saw her here, just moments ago," Claudine explained, "Maybe she went to her room?"

Francis took out his phone and called Andrea again.

"I'll go and check..." Claudine said.

"Shhh!" He put his finger to his lips and listened intently. He could hear Andrea's faint ringtone.

He looked around. Yes, it was coming from the bushes in the back.

He pushed through the branches and followed the sound. Her voicemail came on, so he disconnected and called her number again. Yes. The ringtone came from the left, behind the big bluebeard shrub.

He pulled the branches apart, scratching his hands, and lying on the ground, in a circle of pale white mushrooms, there lay Andrea's ringing cellphone. She was gone.

4

———

ORPHANS AND SPIES

AGENT DELANCEY SAT down on the passenger seat and shut the door. His white shirt was crumpled and his black tie tilted to the side.

"What?" he said to Beatrice, who sat at the steering wheel and watched him closely.

"Your eye," she said.

He didn't want to talk about his eye. "I thought we were in a hurry."

They pulled out of the bureau's underground garage and into the sunny day outside. Pale and sweaty Delancey looked out the window.

"Navy blue is the color of the season," she teased him. "You'll get all the ladies with that handsome bruise."

"What, you want some of the action?" he snapped without even looking at her.

Beatrice laughed, pulled down her window, reached up with her long hand and placed a flasher on the roof. Delancey grimaced at the sound of the siren. Didn't help his headache.

They dashed down the city streets, heading to the eastern suburbs.

"Come on, I should know what happened to my superior," she said. "A jealous husband?"

"Okay," he sighed. "Seeing as you won't get off me otherwise. I was sitting there on the pier, slightly under the calming influence of benzodiazepines, minding my own damn business and analyzing the ebb and flow of the ocean ... next to this street gym or whatever it's called. It was night. And there I see a really nice girl with this alpha male asshole in a suit. You know the kind, thousand-dollar-worth. They're passing by me, and the prick, just like that, jumps on a pull-up bar and does this kind of spin on it, like gymnasts do, to show off to her. Then he jumps off the bar and punches me straight in the face."

"Like that? Unprovoked?"

"Like that."

"Are you sure you didn't say anything beforehand?"

"Now I think of it, I might've said something."

"Andrew..."

"To myself. Or maybe to the girl?"

"Now we're getting there. What was it you said?"

"I asked her 'How's that feel, going out with a circus monkey?'"

"Can't keep your tongue behind your teeth, eh, Chief?"

"I can. But what's the fun?"

"You are a man with a death wish. And as amusing as that can be, it scares the hell out of me."

They grew quiet. Delancey didn't tell her what happened after the man hit him. How the rage had blinded him, how he'd jumped on the young guy like a rabid pit bull, knocked him to the ground and kept kicking him madly, in the stomach, in the head, in the hands as the man tried to cover himself, groaning and begging forgiveness. Then Delancey noticed the girl filming him with her cellphone, crying for him to stop, and he grabbed her phone, smashed it under his shoe and walked away.

He'd really wanted to jump that night. The ocean had

seemed so inviting, the oblivion and solace eternal in its dark depths. But he remembered his job, his defiance to the world, his promise he made that he would remain an obstacle to the Fates' wicked ways until they killed him. Jumping now would render it all void and meaningless. So he just went home and drank himself to sleep.

Suffice to say, the 20mg of Escitalopram and 10mg of Wellbutrin his doctor had him on weren't helping much. There was only one drug in the entire world that made him feel a complete human. And he swore to never touch it again.

"I don't have a death wish," he said finally. "I'm just fucked up in the head."

THE SUN WAS SHINING on the pleasant little family house with a white fence and neatly trimmed lawn. There was a swing, and a sandbox with scattered toys. Only the grim cops, like omens of misfortune, standing by the front door waiting for Delancey and Beatrice, spoiled the bucolic atmosphere of suburban life.

Delancey looked at the name on the mailbox and stopped.

"Wait a moment. Weren't those...?"

"Yes," Beatrice answered. "The Dowleys. Their son was one of the children kidnapped by Ricko Boleani. Five years old."

Delancey looked at her and sighed.

They took the report from the cop at the door and went in. They looked at the two headless bodies sitting on the bloodstained couch in the living room. Beatrice went to the children's room first, and Delancey passed her as she stood at the door, frozen, mute and pale, and he took in the situation.

"Aaaand we have their heads," he said. "The heads of the parents and the head of their child, arranged next to each other on a shelf, facing the room, next to some toys. The headless body of the child is on the bed, lying on its back."

"I have to go outside," Beatrice muttered.

"Wait a second..." Delancey crouched, took a handkerchief from his pocket, and picked up something from the floor.

"What is it?" Beatrice tried not to look at the carnage. He could hear her voice trembling.

"That's the question," Delancey said and showed her what he had in his hand. It looked like a teddy bear, but made of porous black stone, like lava rock or pumice. "A strange toy."

"That's the only thing you find strange here, Andrew? Not that there's someone capable of ... doing that?" She pointed with her chin, trying not to look at the shelf.

"Well..." He looked at the heads and shrugged. "Humans doing what they do."

THEY STOOD OUTSIDE and looked at the white clouds passing in the blue sky like happy fairytale sailboats over the calm suburbia of New Lakoff.

"Tell the cops to scan the house for any prints they can find. I will need an expert opinion from the coroner. Cutting off a head isn't such a clean and easy job. Demands strength and proper tools. Contact all the other families too. Tell Oscar to move them to safe houses and give them protection. I don't believe it's an accident. Life is full of pain, but the family here already had more than their statistical share. Lightning doesn't strike twice like that."

"What about Gabriel and Matt?"

"I'll go and take them to a safe house myself. The one on Flote Street is vacant at the moment, I think."

While Bea turned to the policemen to distribute the orders, Delancey walked a few steps away and sat on a swing. He called Gabriel's number. No answer. So he called the orphanage.

"Is Gabriel West in?" he asked the receptionist.

"Oh ... and who's calling?" answered the woman with a

strange tone in her voice. He frowned and held his phone firmer.

"Senior Agent Andrew Delancey, NBI. The director knows me..."

"Yes, of course... well, there's this thing ... I'm not really allowed to give any information."

"What? What information? I'm just asking you to—"

"I have to go. Goodbye."

Delancey cursed. "What the hell's going on over there?"

He put his phone away and turned to Beatrice.

"We have to split," he said. "I know you can take care of this business here. I'll take a cab."

"Where are you going?"

Dark, lean boys played basketball behind the chain-link fence, screaming obscenities and laughing and applauding good players. Delancey stood next to the fence for a second and looked at their proud faces. Their childhood had been stolen from them. He felt right at home.

He came in through the giant gate unperturbed. The great, dimly lit hall smelled of disinfectants and floor polish. Delancey saw Matt, the one-eyed sad boy, straight away. He stood by the window, looking outside. One of the caregivers, a young woman in a woolen sweater with a nametag, stood next to him.

"Hey, mister!" he heard someone calling from behind. A mustachioed janitor trotted towards him, angry at both Delancey and himself for not noticing him sooner. "Where do you think you're going? Can I help you?"

"Yeah, you can go away," Delancey said and walked up to Matt. He kneeled and touched his shoulders. Matt turned around and stared at him.

"Hi, buddy. Recognize me? Agent Delancey, from the other night. The bad guy almost ended me, but we managed, eh?"

"Sir?" the caregiver said carefully and exchanged glances with the janitor. "Who are you, exactly—?"

"That's okay," he answered without looking at her. "Matt, little buddy, do you happen to know where your brother is? We think he might be in danger. Where is Gabriel, do you know?"

"Yes," Matt said in a little voice. Delancey laughed as the caregiver gasped in surprise.

"Matt, you're speaking!" she said.

"He had to go away," Matt continued. "Because this man wants to catch him."

The little boy pointed down the corridor. Delancey looked.

The orphanage's director, a big blond man in glasses, stood in his office door staring at them. Behind him was a tall man with a long face resembling a Doberman, his hair cut short, and he was wearing an elegant cashmere coat. Delancey knew a CAISA agent when he saw one.

"Wait for me, buddy," he whispered to Matt. He stood and walked up to the director's office.

"Agent Delancey, this is—" the director started speaking, but Delancey interrupted him:

"A man outside his jurisdiction, bound by our local city laws, and staying here on the rights of a guest. Am I correct?"

Two more tall, intimidating men walked out of the director's office. They were built like gorillas and had faces to match.

"My jurisdiction is a curious case, Senior Agent Delancey," the Doberman-face man slowly said with a cold smile, "In that it can be suddenly extended. As long as your superiors wish to remain in good relations with CAISA. Jack Crowe."

Crowe extended a hand, which Delancey ignored. He lowered it and his smile died on his lips. He looked back to his smirking colleagues, then back to Delancey. "I understand ours is not a love at first sight."

"You're interested in Boleani's case?" Delancey asked. "If so, why not come to me? I was the main guy on that. You know our address."

"Your address? Oh, we know most of them. But we're not so much interested in the case itself. We deal with our share of murderous psychopaths, as I'm sure you're aware of. It's the details that caught our curiosity."

"What details?"

"Well..." The CAISA agent stared at his shiny brown shoes for a while. "You know the investigation didn't go the usual way. Including its finale at the airport. One might say it was even supernatural."

"You believe in the supernatural, Agent Crowe?"

"Not supernatural? Then maybe the better word would be ... special? Yes? And we're very interested in special things. That's why we're special agents. I don't really care about your work, no doubt very useful locally. I'd just like to meet the big brother of that boy over there."

"I don't think that's necessary."

"Please let me decide that. If you know where Gabriel West is at the moment, I'd be grateful if you shared that information with me."

"I don't think you can give me orders."

"Is that so?" An evil flicker of light appeared in Crowe's eyes. "CAISA is class zero government agency. The last time I checked, NBI didn't need class zero to look out for city dogs shitting on sidewalks, so..."

"The last time I checked, officially you have the same authority over me as a dog shitting on a sidewalk—that is, zero," muttered Delancey.

"That could change, though," Crowe noticed. "And then you could have problems."

"Listen, Mr. Crowe," Delancey put his heavy hand on the agent's shoulder. The man was a good foot taller than him, but Delancey didn't let him feel any superior. "You came here, all the way from Lanaken onto my turf, sniffing for some sensationalist gossip you overheard from one of your lackeys here. You should fire him. Gabriel West is a poor boy suffering from delusions, and you and your agency are ridiculous for believing this bullshit. So my advice is, go to your Area 11, uncover an alien carcass or two and make some sweet, sweet, love to him. That would be much more 'special' than anything you can find in Los Maines."

Delancey gave Jack Crowe one last smile, squeezed his shoulder, then turned away and went back to Matt.

"Area 11 is Air Force, not us," Crowe said, but Delancey ignored him.

He knelt next to Matt.

"Now you're talking, I'm so happy to hear that," he whispered to him. "Do you know where Gabriel is?"

Matt just shrugged.

"You're not saying. As long as you don't tell it to them..." Delancey gestured with his chin to Crowe. "That's fine by me, little buddy. And now we need to go."

He grabbed Matt's hand.

"Hey, hey, hey, you can't do that!" Crowe came up to them.

"Of course I can," Delancey said. "As of now, he's under witness protection. You're afraid you're going to lose your bait?"

"The boy stays here," Crowe said.

"Fuck you."

Crowe nodded to his two large companions.

Each one grabbed Delancey under his shoulders.

He kicked the one to the left in the groin, and attempted to punch the one to the right, but the other goon grabbed him from behind.

"Please, there's no need for that! The children are watching!" the orphanage director cried. "Agent Delancey, I'm afraid we have to listen to the gentlemen here. They have a document..."

"They're holding you hostage at your own place!" Delancey said. "The boy's not safe here!"

Matt pursed his little lips, covered his ears, clenched his one eye, and began shaking his head violently.

"Hush, Matt ... hush..." His caregiver knelt next to Matt and embraced him. She looked up at Delancey and shook her head.

Delancey nodded and stopped screaming. He just looked with hate at Crowe, who called someone on his phone.

"Hi, ma'am, it's Agent Crowe," he said to someone on the line. "We have problems with one of your men ... Agent Delancey ... yes, of course—"

He handed Delancey his phone with a wide grin. The two big spies let him go. Delancey shrugged off their heavy hands, adjusted his jacket, and took the phone.

"Hello?"

"Andrew! What the hell are you doing there?" he heard the angry voice of his new boss, Melissa Tornatore.

"I wanted to take the young West into the witness protection program," he said, looking at Crowe's malicious smile. "I'm worried about his safety..."

"Permission denied."

"Excuse me?"

"You are obligated to assist Mr. Crowe's in his duties," she snapped. "And see me in my office, ASAP."

"Ma'am..."

"Enough."

And she disconnected. He was holding to Crowe's phone for a second, murdering the smiling secret agent with his stare, and eventually handed it back to him.

"I'll be back," he said and left the building.

Outside, the cops he had called beforehand were already in place.

One of them approached Delancey.

"Agent?" he said.

"Yes," said Delancey. "Set up a post here. I want the whole place under surveillance, twenty-four seven, at least three armed officers, one at the door, the others patrolling the area."

He walked down the street and he felt his phone vibrate in his pocket. Looked at the screen.

Incoming Call: Gabriel West.

5

LAST SUNDAY

GABRIEL OPENED HIS EYES. He saw the pale sunlight on the Styrofoam tiles of the ceiling and he remembered why he was so uncomfortable and his back hurt. The drugstore.

He sat up on the cardboard and glanced at his cell phone, plugged into a wall socket, charging.

"Li, what time is it?"

"Eleven thirty-two," answered the demon of his phone, Li, who looked like a thin, tall teenager in a baseball cap with a symbol of a dragon. "Also, Andrew Delancey called."

Gabriel groaned and got to his feet. He looked around for Maurice but the demon was nowhere to be seen, so he shook his wristband.

"Maurice, come out."

Maurice appeared instantly, with his signature crooked smile.

"Good morning. Had a good sleep?"

"I'm totally sore." Gabriel gathered his things into his backpack and the many pockets of his cargo pants. "Let's get out of here."

He went back to the courtyard of his apartment building. The sunlight was white and cold, lending it an unearthly feel.

He immediately realized something was wrong: next to the bike rack there stood Giovanni, the demon of his bicycle, upset and gesturing to him.

One look was enough to understand what had happened: somebody had stolen both wheels. The bike stood on its metal prongs, still chained to the rack, useless.

"Cursed *diavoli!*" Giovanni lamented. "Three teenagers, with primitive faces and swearing so much your ears would wither! They tried to pick the lock, and when they failed, one of them said, 'Good wheels, let's sling them!' Gabriel, I'm so sorry, there's nothing I could do!"

"Great start to a new day," Maurice commented.

Just then, Li appeared next to them.

"There's an incoming call from the orphanage," he said.

Gabriel immediately reached for his phone and answered the call.

"Yes?"

"Hello! This is the telephone from the orphanage calling!" a female voice whispered with urgency. "I'm the one you commanded to inform you whenever there's trouble!"

"I know, I know! What's going on?"

"There was another stranger in our halls. The men in rain-coats, who looked for you yesterday, addressed him as Agent Delancey! He tried to take Matt away but the men didn't let him!"

"Okay. What's the situation now?"

"The men from yesterday are talking in the director's office and waiting for you. And the new man, this Agent Delancey, asked Matt about you as well! And he brought three policemen with him, who right now are sitting outside and eating Chinese food from paper boxes, while this Delancey fellow is walking away from our orphanage!"

"And Matt?"

"He's in the common room, drawing. He's drawing a comic. A common room lamp told the hall lamps, and they told me."

"Good. So, he's safe?"

"Yes, yes. Nothing extraordinary. But the stranger talked to him, and scared him, as I said, and there are those new policemen outside ... it was enough of odd happenings we thought you need to be notified!"

"You did well. Keep me informed whenever something new happens. Understood?"

"Ombudsman, I understand and I will obey your commands," replied the voice. "Now I end the call, unless there are more matters you wish to discuss...?"

"Li?" Gabriel turned to the demon of his phone. "Get me Delancey."

He waited for a few signals until Delancey answered the phone.

"Good to hear you, son," he heard the familiar voice. "Are you in town?"

"Yes. You wanted to take Matt away from the orphanage?"

"Let's meet ASAP. I'll text you the address. Can you do that?"

Gabriel and Maurice looked at each other.

"See you there," Gabriel said, and disconnected. He heard a ping and saw a text with an address.

"Are you sure we can trust him?" Maurice asked. "And how do we get there, what with Giovanni's wheels missing?"

"I have an idea."

He walked across the parking lot until he found his mother's car. There was a stack of parking tickets all over its windshield, and a big yellow wheel clamp embraced its front left wheel.

"Gabriel!" cried a voice with a French accent, and a tall man in a leather jacket appeared next to the car. He had a thin mustache and his shirt was unbuttoned at his hairy chest. "I'm Pierre, the demon of your mother's car! I carried you to school, and Matt to kindergarten, and your mother to work every day, and now something happened and I'm left here for dogs to pee on, and for street cops to present me with parking tickets! Now, see what they did to my wheel! What's going on? Please, tell me!"

"That's a long story," Gabriel said. He pointed at the clamp and made the Sign of the Covenant. "Let go of that wheel, you asshole."

GABRIEL DIDN'T TALK MUCH with his mother's car as they drove through the city. He gave perfunctory answers to its questions. Mother had left to a different city, he told the Car. No one knew when she would be back.

The address Delancey had given him was in the Lakoff district, so they drove past his school, Rosewater High. He was going to skip even more classes than he thought. He looked from the driver's seat at the students in the schoolyard, hoping to see the familiar face of Martin or maybe Andrea.

Pierre didn't have GPS, so Li had to help him find the address from Delancey. They turned into a quiet, bland housing development, with identical single-family homes and lawns. Finally, Gabriel saw a police cruiser and Delancey's familiar silhouette in the driveway of one house and told the car to pull over.

"No, no, no," Beatrice said, coming out of the house as she saw the two of them. "I know what you want. He shouldn't be here. He's been through enough."

"Bea, let us in," Delancey said. "Together we can solve that. And prevent it from happening ever again."

"He's still a child, Andrew."

"There was a child in this house, as well. And there are more of them who can meet the same fate."

"It's wrong."

"Beatrice," Gabriel said quietly. "I killed my own mother."

She was silent for a while, then she sighed and shook her head. "It's not pretty what happened here, Gabriel."

"That's alright," the boy said. "I can make it."

"Are the bodies still there?" Delancey asked.

"Of course not. We were getting ready to leave, as well."

"Tell the cops to go outside."

GABRIEL STOOD in the living room. The only thing left from the bodies were dark stains and blots on the couch where they were found. Beatrice and Delancey waited in silence next to him, and looked on as he listened to the demons of the place.

Eventually, he grimaced and hid his face in his hands.

"God damn," he said. "God damn."

"Gabe?" Delancey said. "You okay, son?"

Gabriel looked at him. His face was changed.

"Who are they?" he whispered. "The two killers in white?"

"Two killers in white," Delancey repeated. "Now that's the first I've heard of them. You need to tell us what happened here."

And Gabriel began speaking, in a detached, resigned voice.

"It was yesterday around 5PM. The front door unlocked on command and two men with long blond hair, dressed in white, entered the house. The phones refused to work as mother and father tried to call the police. The strangers just looked at them with a smile. The child was afraid and the mother comforted it. Father kept repeating for the strangers to leave. They asked questions about what happened when Ricko Boleani's basement had been raided. The family said they didn't know anything. Then, one of the strangers took the father in his arms and started to dance with him all through the room, and father told him to please stop. Then, they ordered the whole family to dance. Mother, father, and child tried to dance, crying and afraid, while the two sat on the couch, commenting on who danced the best and giving scores." Gabriel tried to swallow some saliva through his contracted throat. He rubbed his eyes. "Then, one of the two took the child upstairs to show him a trick. The second one told the parents to sit on the couch, quickly gave them injections after which they couldn't get up or move. He took out a dark, long knife. And, well ... he cut off their heads alive. And the demons here don't know what happened upstairs, so..."

Gabriel looked around for the staircase, found it, and started walking in its direction.

"I don't think you should—" said Beatrice, but he already went upstairs.

"Where's the boy's room?" they heard him ask an invisible demon.

Delancey wanted to follow him, but Beatrice grabbed his elbow.

"We're damaging him," she said. "It's too much even for a grown-up who's not desensitized, like us. We have no right."

"Well, do you have a better plan for him? He's lost for life, Bea. After all he's been through, there's no coming back."

She stared for a long while into Delancey's gray eyes and slowly shook her head.

"He doesn't have to end up like you, Andrew," she said quietly. She let go of his elbow and went upstairs to join Gabriel.

He stood in the child's room, listening to a demon.

"This knife..." he whispered. "Maurice? Is it possible?"

"What's going on here?" Delancey asked, coming into the room.

Gabriel took a while before answering, collecting his thoughts.

"Where is it?" he asked a demon. On the floor, he found the teddy bear turned to gray stone. "The same as my apartment," he whispered to himself.

Delancey raised his voice. "Gabriel? Can you tell me what's going on?" Gabriel finally noticed him.

"Well ... the man told the boy he'd show him a trick. And he took his toy away from him and killed its demon with his knife. So the toy turned to this ... strange stone, all dead. It's how my apartment looks now."

"So it's the same people."

"If they're people."

They stared at each other.

"And then?" Delancey said finally.

"He killed the boy. The same way the one downstairs offed his parents," Gabriel said simply, and wiped his eyes with a short, angry move, because he didn't want to be seen crying. "Is that it?" he said suddenly. "Are they targeting Boleani's victims?"

"We don't know that yet," Delancey said.

Gabriel grabbed his arm. "We have to hide Matt. Now!"

"Well, there's some of my men there..."

Gabriel laughed bitterly. "Three cops? Against two Ombudsmen? Are you joking? We almost died, all of us, trying to stop one. And those two seem to be much more powerful. Climbing walls, killing demons—"

"I'm afraid I can't take Matt from there, Gabriel," Delancey said.

"Why?"

"The CAISA agents want him to stay there. And they contacted my boss. I have to be a good dog and do what they tell me."

Gabriel considered that for a while.

"If so, I have to go where he is and be with him," he said quietly.

"Then you'll be the one against the two Ombudsmen. Correct?"

"Better me than three cops."

"I'll send more."

"What about CAISA?" Beatrice said. "They'll grab you the moment they see you. Those guys train with Gurkhas and Green

Berets. If they don't like you, they smear some nerve agent on your doorknob and you die of heart attack in your own bed. You don't mess with CAISA."

"I can manage them," answered Gabriel.

"They're military intelligence. We have no power over them. They can bring in the whole army to shoot a cannonade each time they want to fart. And if they so much as catch wind that we're helping you, it will be over."

Gabriel kept quiet. Then he said finally:

"So, what should we do?"

"Let's not panic. Okay?" Delancey said. "At the moment, the boy has more protection than anyone in this city. Both CAISA and our men. I'll ask Ruslan to add some of his crew to that mix. Right now, let's finish the job here. Then we'll decide. Let's start with the facial composite."

Beatrice gave Gabriel a tablet with a special app. There was a face on the screen and he could switch eyes, noses and mouths by tapping on arrows.

"Tell me what they looked like," Gabriel said to the demons. "Let's start with the first one."

"They were very similar," said the demon of the clock that hung on the wall. "I would even think they were twins."

"Yes!" agreed the demon of the living room table. "Only one of them had this mole on his cheek. And he spoke with a lisp."

"So the faces would be identical, right?" Gabriel asked. "Let's try and recreate it. The shape?"

"Oh, less round. Much longer," the demons pointed out. "Lips thinner. Longer nose and more narrow. The eyes, big, big, and long eyelashes. Thin eyebrows. And long hair, blond hair. To their shoulders."

"Like that?" Gabriel showed the screen to the demons.

"It's them," hissed the demon of the clock.

Gabriel looked on the tablet one more time. He saw a handsome face of a young man, one could say very delicate, almost feminine. A total opposite of Ricko Boleani's aggressive mug.

He gave the tablet back to Beatrice.

"That's them. According to the demons."

Delancey nodded with satisfaction.

"See? I was right about having Gabriel here. Tell Oscar to post it on our social feeds."

6

———

ASK THE ROADS

THEY STOOD in the afternoon on a road that went through the suburbs, next to the Dowleys' house. All around them, identical houses spread into the distance, each with a different car in the driveway, with children going round on their tricycles, automatic sprinklers waking now that the sun was low.

A group of ten-year-olds passed them, racing their bikes down the road, on their after-school adventures.

"We need to know how they came here," Delancey said.

Gabriel looked around to find the right demon to ask.

"Come out," he said, and made a sweeping gesture with his hand.

The lawns around them swarmed with a pale, blue-skinned crowd.

"The two men in white, how did they come here?" he asked. "Did anybody see that?"

"They had a motorbike!" the demons talked one over another. "They rode a motorbike here."

"Hey, Road, do you remember when they came here?" Gabriel asked.

The demon of the asphalt road was the epitome of the stay-at-home mom from the 1950s, with a worried face, curly hair, flowery dress.

"I'm the road your weary father takes on his way back from work, thinking about a warm dinner with his close ones. I'm the calm road your mother crosses without having to look left or right, to talk with the neighbors and bring them a cake. The road which seems to stretch so far when you're a little child and makes you think about the grown-up future in the wide world to which I lead. Not often two men come here on a fast sport motorbike. I see SUVs much more often. Not often do they stop by my side to enter one of the homes. Not often they leave with droplets of blood on their white suits to go away fast in the direction of the city."

"I'll take that as a yes," Gabriel said. "Did you see where they came from, and where they left to?"

"They got on me turning from the big road, the one that boasts streetlights and four lanes, the one that goes and goes straight to the city center of Los Maines. And the same way they left."

Gabriel turned to Delancey and Beatrice.

"The two of them came and left on a sport bike, arriving from the main road..."

"Sennhauer Street," Bea said. "Let's go and ask there, it's not far."

They walked down the road between family houses and well-trimmed lawns and hedges, the locals staring at them from their porches.

They arrived at the intersection and Gabriel called out the demon of Sennhauer Street: a working dad, wearing a shirt-no-tie and a casual suit. He seemed to be in a hurry.

"We're looking for two men dressed in white, on a sport motorbike," Gabriel said. "They were here yesterday. Have you seen them?"

"Son, you must be joking!" the Sennhauer Street said. "You

think I have time for that? You realize how many people drive here every day? I have four lanes, I go all way from Constanza to Los Maines, Old Port. And I'm supposed to know each and every biker?"

"No need to get all worked up, okay?" Gabriel said and turned to the agents. "The street doesn't remember them."

"But I do," said the speed bump in the road, and its demon appeared before Gabriel, a neurasthenic with dark circles under his eyes. "Look at that street, acting all haughty just because it has damn four lanes. My work is much more important, I'm small, but I keep my watch so no idiot son who borrows Dad's car is speeding, and no damn midlife-crisis uncle in his Ferrari goes too fast on a residential road and God forbid hits a child or some other peaceful inhabitant of this housing estate!"

"That's enough," Gabriel sighed. "Get to the point."

"I have no way of knowing where they came from, but I have the bike's make and numbers," the Bump said. "I always remember such details when I see a stranger in our peaceful community."

"What was it, then?"

"It was a white motorbike with 'Ducate' written in golden letters on its fuel tank," said the Bump. "And the license plate was WXI85210."

"White Ducate, license WXI85210," Gabriel repeated, and Beatrice noted it down in her phone and immediately started calling someone. "Thank you. You can go back into your totems now."

The demons disappeared and Gabriel looked at Delancey. "Well, seems we have something."

"Registered as stolen yesterday morning," Beatrice said, disconnecting her call. "In Redwood. I have a patrol going to the owner right now. Apparently, it was stolen from where it was parked, without the key."

"Redwood," Delancey repeated, and gave her a heavy stare.

"What's in Redwood?" Gabriel asked.

"Well ... the hospital which was the first place we moved all the children rescued from Boleani's basement."

There was a short silence, suddenly broken by a big delivery truck turning into the road, huffing and puffing its engine.

"I'll ask the Redwood hospital if they noticed anything out of the ordinary. Tell the traffic division to have an eye out for the bike," Delancey said.

Beatrice nodded. "Of course."

"And I'm going where my place is," Gabriel said.

They looked at him.

"And that is...?"

"Where I can protect my brother."

They watched him get into Pierre the car and drive away.

"Does he even have a driver's license?" Beatrice asked with a frown.

"Technically, he's not driving," Delancey said. "I guess it's more like taking a cab."

He sat on a curb, got out his telephone and found the contact for the Redwood hospital.

"What am I going to ask them? 'Have you seen anything strange?' And who exactly do I ask?" He looked at Beatrice with a sour face. "There's only one proper way to do it."

"I know," she sighed. "Let's hit the road."

With the heavy traffic and all the people coming back from work, it was an hour's drive from Lakoff to Redwood. Delancey sat in the passenger seat and looked from time to time at Beatrice's strong thighs stretching her blue jeans as she pressed the pedals. He asked how her husband was.

"We're not together anymore," she said without much emotion.

"Bea, no! You were so good together."

"Yes, we were so good together that I screwed you after work."

"Okay, point taken, but that was only physical, no?"

She didn't answer for a while. Finally, she shook her head slowly. "You're such an idiot, Agent Delancey."

"Come on, what happened between you two?"

"I couldn't be with him anymore. I understood it wasn't fair."

"So, are you seeing someone?"

"Actually I am."

"Oh?"

"Linda, from communications."

"Really?" Surprised, Delancey looked up from her legs up to her face. "But she's a…"

"Woman."

"I didn't know you switched sides."

"A human touch is a human touch, Agent Delancey."

He shrugged and looked out the window.

"I hope it wasn't me who soured you to our gender. Can you believe this traffic?"

THE HOSPITAL at Redwood was a surprisingly-large seven-story building surrounded with poplars. Delancey and Beatrice asked the parking security for the stolen motorbike, but they hadn't seen it. Nobody saw anything worth recounting in the last few days. It was only when they asked the receptionist inside that he remembered something.

"Yes, of course … yesterday afternoon at, I don't know, one? Two p.m.? They made quite an entrance. Two tall guys, handsome like movie stars, wearing white suits. Hard not to notice them."

"What did they want?"

"Now that is a bit strange. You see, one of them came up and asked me if this was the hospital where the children saved from the Stellen Kidnapper were put. I thought they were from some kind of entertainment industry. Like I said, movie people, looking for info about the case, so I said yes. I thought they wanted to interview me or something."

"And did they?"

"A strange thing happened. The other one put his hand on my computer, like that..." The receptionist moved his palm along the back of his laptop's screen. "And he said: 'Tell me everything.' So I asked what exactly interests them, but they were, like, not listening to me anymore? They stared at the floor and nodded. I said, 'Hello, is anybody there?' And they looked at each other, smiled, and left."

"Did anyone else have contact with them?"

"I think Carina saw them. Carina!" the receptionist bellowed at a stout woman in a black security uniform, who sat by the entrance watching something on her phone.

She removed her headphones and looked at them askance.

"You remember those two guys from yesterday?"

"Oh sure I remember. Hot pieces of ass, you know?" She laughed and shook her head.

"These guys here are from NBI, asking about them. You remember if they said anything or something?"

"Just one thing, when they were leaving. One said something to the other."

"What was it?" Delancey asked the woman.

"He said..." She frowned, trying to remember the exact words. "Oh, yes. 'Let the fun commence.'"

7

———

ASK THE DARKNESS

EVENING WAS FALLING over Los Maines, and Gabriel told his dead mother's car to drive him to the old district, where the orphanage was located. He sat in the driver's seat while the car drove itself, looking at the streets of the city where he had grown up in an ordinary world, without demons and murders and magic from beyond.

He stopped at a small, dark grocery store and bought some bread rolls, cheese, dried sausage, milk chocolate, and a bottle of water. He paid the man whose face was obscured by all the lottery ads sticked to the glass.

He parked the car by a house next to the orphanage. He stood for some time, looking at a police car and several cops at the gate. Seemed everything was alright.

Then he went to an old brownstone on the other side of the street and asked the gray, crumbling stairs:

"Any vacant apartments here?"

"No."

He went to the next house down the street.

"Any empty apartments here?" he said quietly to the door.

"Why yes, indeed," it answered. "Since the death of Mrs. Kurek, let her soul rest in peace, her apartment stands empty.

Only her adult children come here at times to quarrel bitterly about inheritance."

"What number is that?"

"Apartment 4A. Fourth floor."

"Let me in."

The apartment was dark and stuffy; it smelled of dust and old people's medicines. His footsteps creaking on the wooden floor, Gabriel opened the windows in the rooms on both sides of the hall for some fresh air, and the wind lifted the ancient curtains in its intermittent gusts.

He plugged a drone charging station into a socket and turned on Captain Nakamura's drone.

"*Konnichiwa*, Captain," he said.

"Ready for orders, Commander!" answered Nakamura, saluting in his pilot's leather cap.

"Here's a charging station for you to use when needed. Go and keep watch over the orphanage. Let me know when you see anyone suspicious. Especially ... two men, dressed in white, travelling on a sport motorbike."

"Aye, aye, sir!" Nakamura turned on his rotors and with a buzz flew out the dining room window.

Gabriel sat there at an old table and took the food out of the bags. He hadn't eaten since yesterday, but felt no hunger. He knew he had to eat to have energy for whatever lay ahead.

He looked at a couch by the wall, covered with a checkered blanket.

"Hey. Any small creatures here I should know about?" he asked the table's demon.

The Table, an old, wrinkled man in an elegant waiter's attire —white shirt, black vest, a bow tie—scoffed at him in a dignified manner.

"Excuse me? What do you mean, you uninvited visitor at this late hour?"

"I mean bedbugs," Gabriel clarified. "Old people don't notice such things."

"Well, excuse me! Maybe the Andersons have bedbugs, the unkempt swine, but not here, no sir! Back when our owner lived, she had the whole apartment cleaned every Wednesday, and we never had any problems with vermin or any other infestation..."

"Whoa, sorry for asking," Gabriel said.

It was already dark outside. He suddenly felt very lonely in this strange apartment. He took out his phone, thought for a second, and chose the number of Martin, his best friend from school, but disconnected the moment he heard Martin's "Hello?"

He couldn't imagine himself talking to Martin now. He was a completely different person in a different world. There were no more bridges leading to the past.

He stared at the couch some more. He really didn't want to sleep here, in some dead old lady's rooms. He grabbed several pillows and two blankets, left his things in the apartment, and went up the narrow, windowless staircase, all the way up to the top floor, where he quietly ordered a small wooden door to open and let him go out to the roof.

On the roof, under the open night sky, full of clouds racing by and obscuring and revealing the moon and distant stars, he propped some pillows under a chimney and sat down, leaning himself against them. He covered himself with a blanket, and looked at the orphanage, pinkish in the light of the streetlamp, its several windows lit in celadon and the rest already black. He watched as the small disc of Captain Nakamura circled the perimeter and landed to rest on one of the orphanage's gables.

He was as close to his brother as he could be, to protect him from the two human monsters in white—if anybody were able to face them at all.

He saw Maurice standing on the distant corner of the roof, listening to something intently, nodding and whispering.

"What's up, Maurice?" he asked quietly as the demon returned to him. "Did you learn anything from your secret sources?"

"I asked for any information about Princes they could find."

"You have something?"

"Nobody ever seen any of them in this country. But there was talk of their kind in the south, in Chile, Argentina, the islands. The knives are called Kanchaks. They can kill demons. The Princes can climb all walls, and all things created by man have to listen to them ... and here's the thing. They don't need to show the Sign of the Covenant, like Ombudsmen. We just have to listen to whatever they say. Or they kill us. Like they killed your apartment."

"Do you think they can kill the whole city?" Gabriel whispered. "Like killing its spirit?"

Maurice lowered his head and thought for a while.

"No. I don't think that would be possible. Look, even the demon of an apartment building is huge and strong. Not to mentions spirits of cities! It'd be weird if a small knife like that could take them out."

"It would be weird?"

"Right."

"But you don't know for sure."

"I don't. But I never heard of such a case. I mean, try and kill a whale with a knife."

Gabriel sighed.

"What do you think they want? Revenge for Ricko's death? They're his friends, maybe?"

Maurice chortled. "I'm sure Ricko Boleani had lots of friends," he answered. "Being the life of the party he was."

But Gabriel didn't laugh. "We nearly died fighting him. Imagine what the two of them can do. Maybe I should take Matt and steal a plane, fly somewhere ... to a distant island maybe, where they can't find us."

"One, Matt happens to be in a building occupied by secret agents who want to lock you in a cage and take you to a government lab…"

"I'd be much happier to take on them than those two fucking Princes."

"And two…" Maurice shrugged. "Well, you know Los Maines. You know the language. Foreign demons may not understand you. There's the language barrier. And also, here is where your allies are. Friends, if you will."

Gabriel looked at him for a while. Then, he turned his head away.

"I don't know what to do," he said simply.

"How about you sleep?" Maurice said. "Ask yourself what you should do and go to sleep."

"How do you mean?"

"Ah, I don't know. Just something I heard once," Maurice smiled. "At times of turmoil and uncertainty, you should ask yourself for help and go to sleep. The sleep will bring you the answer. The darkness within you is smarter than you are."

Gabriel leered and shook his head.

Hey you, darkness within me, he thought. *What can I do? Where can I turn for help?*

He wrapped himself tighter in the blanket, looked up at the stars and the silver clouds. He thought he could see a blinking light moving across the sky, a satellite or a space station.

He closed his eyes and, breath after breath, fell deeper and deeper into sleep.

The dream snatched him in an instant. He was in a stuffy, cramped space, with vibrating metal walls and full of electrical hum. The light was dim there and fluctuating like a stroboscope set to a very fast speed. There were no windows. He saw a metal locker in the wall. He was afraid of what was inside. But despite himself, his hands not listening to his orders, he reached out and opened the metal door.

His father was inside. Stuffed into the locker, standing there, very thin and pale, looking at Gabriel with horror. And Gabriel saw there was a thick black tube of corrugated rubber stuck into his father's mouth, leading to a hole in the wall behind.

He woke up with a scream.

The echo of his scream rang over the roofs and crumbled walls of the brownstone houses.

It was dawn.

Gabriel lay for a second on his back, staring at the milky, clouded sky of the new day, trying to understand what he'd seen. He shivered but he didn't know if the cold was the cause, or the dream.

He sat up.

"Gabriel?" Maurice said with concern.

"We're going," the boy answered and gathered the pillows and blankets.

"Will you tell me what—?" Maurice said as they walked down the street in a brisk pace.

"Pierre! Open up!" Gabriel snapped when they reached his mother's car.

He got inside and shut the door. The demon of the car appeared in the passenger seat next to him.

"Pierre, did you know my father?" he asked the demon.

Pierre pouted and shrugged. It was obvious he didn't like the subject.

"Your mother deserves someone better. Even with her driving skills, the lack of which I attribute more to her artistic nature..."

"She worked as a cleaner," Gabriel said. "What artistic nature?"

"Sometimes children aren't the best judges of their parents, whose rich inner life is hidden from their offspring and revealed only in moments of solitude, like, let's say, a beautiful and almost professional-quality singing during a car drive," Pierre answered dryly. "But will you tell me what happened to her? Why doesn't she drive me anymore?"

Gabriel felt a prick of pain in his heart.

"I told you, she had to leave," he said finally. "Tell me what you know about my father."

"A dry man, always preoccupied with his thoughts," Pierre answered. "I would see him now and then, back when we lived in a perfectly good little house, not that slum. He paid your mother much too little attention in my opinion."

"Do you know where he worked?"

"*Oh la la!* Fine number! His own son doesn't even know where his pa worked," Pierre pointed out with malicious smile.

"You know jack shit about it. He just had a job he couldn't tell us about. And he had to leave often. We loved each other, and my mother loved him. She was never herself after he left. She was depressed, and couldn't hold a well-paying job, and had to start cleaning houses and offices to make ends meet."

Pierre seemed offended with this version of the story.

"Well, if you know so much, why are you asking me? I'm just a stupid little French car."

"I'm asking you, and you're answering, because I'm an Ombudsman and you're a demon, who will listen to me to honor the Covenant."

"Okay!" Pierre yelled. "*Sacre bleu!* Then ask!"

"Did you hear my mother talk about something that could give you any idea of what my dad did for a job?"

Pierre thought for a while.

"Not openly, no. But ... whenever she spoke about it, like maybe on a phone, or to a friend she was giving a lift, there was an air of secrecy." Pierre's French "r" made it sound like "eh ev sikhesee." "It was always things like 'They made him go some-where,' or 'Can't they let you stay with us some more?'"

"Sounds like government work," Maurice said.

"Or mafia," added Gabriel. "In both cases, I know who I should ask for help."

He took out his phone.

"Li, call the Telephone at the orphanage and ask her if everything's fine. Then call Captain Nakamura to continue patrolling the perimeter. Pierre? Start the engine. We're going."

"Gabriel," said Maurice, "will you please tell me—?"

"The dream gave me the answer, just as you said. I have to find our father! I always wanted to do that. Now I have the powers. How could he leave us in such a world where they just barge in at 5 p.m. Sunday and cut off your head? He's our dad."

"You dreamed about your father?"

"It's obvious, that's what I have to do now. I took away Matt's mother from him. Now I will give him back his father. I owe him that! He will take care of him."

"And you?"

Gabriel shrugged.

"I don't need anyone to take care of me."

8

LOST GIRL

At Bureau's headquarters, Delancey left the bathroom stall with a new spring in his step and a tingle in his nostrils. He had had a terrible night, panic attacks returning wave after wave, despite his daily antidepressants and then some benzos to boot. He came to work in the morning sleepy and shivering, in a full sweat, had to avoid Beatrice with her concerned questions, and luckily remembered a small bag of cocaine he had stashed in his desk drawer. It wasn't so great. Nothing was after visiting the huge peaceful grazing lands of Atroposine, outside of which life seemed a dreary waiting room before inevitable death, but it made him able to face another day at work.

He walked down the corridor and saw his two new agents in the bullpen, Oscar Malkov and Pete Bersens. He got them to replace the departed Raymond Ayser. Beatrice and Delancey couldn't decide on one, so they hired both. The twenty-six year-old Oscar seemed quite innocent and fragile, with blond hair and fair complexion, but that didn't stop him from finishing the academy with a ninety-seven percent grade, unheard of in years, and his gentle constitution didn't prevent him from excelling in pathology and criminal medicine. He was a joy to be around, always joking and helpful.

Pete, thirty-two, bulky and black haired, started off as a regular street cop in Rektov, the most dangerous district of Los Maines, with violent crimes rate 789% higher than the national average, with many weeks in a row where each day brought a new homicide. Pete made promotion after promotion at his station. He wasn't as talkative as Oscar, but when he did speak, he left everyone impressed with his sharp reasoning and no-nonsense attitude. He was strong like a bull and driven like an ox, and almost single-handedly led his station to smash the sex-trafficking gang that had ruled Rektov since 2009. Beatrice snatched him up just before he made a promotion to the chief deputy of his precinct.

Delancey liked to think of the two guys as his personal yin and yang.

He nodded at them but didn't stop to chat. He went straight to his office, sat at his desk, and called the traffic division about the white Ducate motorbike.

"We don't have anything yet," came the answer. "The police in Redwood are cooperating with us, but so far no luck."

"Funny, with all those new street cameras you bought on the taxpayers' dime..." Delancey said.

"Spare yourself, Andrew. It's nine in the morning."

"Oh, you're right, too early to even pretend you're working," Delancey snapped, and disconnected.

"Bea!" he called.

"Andy! Nice to see you in a good mood for a change," she said, standing in the door.

"The families. Anything to report after the night?"

"Nothing. All safe and sound in their temporary homes. Some of them asked if the children can go to their scheduled therapy sessions today..."

"Sure. If they buy armored cars and a squad of fully armed marines to protect the therapy center, I can't see why not."

"Got it."

"Can you believe we get the most violent homicide in years, and it means something when you live here, and the fucking traffic jerks can't even locate one extremely specific motorbike."

During his rant, Beatrice looked around his new office with a strange expression on her face.

"What?" he asked finally.

"This place looks exactly like on the day you came in."

"What, was I supposed to ruin it? Shit on the carpet?"

"I mean, don't you have any need to personalize the space somewhat? Like, order some movie posters, put up your police diploma...?"

"Why?"

"To make it more homey. This place looks like from an IKEA catalogue."

Delancey stared at her blankly, and it was obvious he didn't understand what she meant. Beatrice chortled.

"Forget it. Didn't want to fry your brain. There's someone to see you."

"What? Now?"

"Francis Bay."

"And who the fuck is that?"

"Ask our boss, Mrs. Tornatore. The meeting came through her PA."

Delancey sighed, combed his hair back with his hands, then wiped them on his pants, because they got sticky with hair gel.

"Bring him in, please."

Francis was a shadow of a man, deadly pale, with dark bags under his bloodshot eyes. Years of corporate habit still kept strong apparently, because he still wore an expensive suit and a well-pressed shirt.

Delancey pointed to the chair on the other side of his desk.

As Francis sat down, Delancey noticed his guest's hands trembled. *We make a nice couple*, he thought.

"Mrs. Tornatore says you're the right man to see about my problem," Francis said.

"I'm happy to hear that," Delancey replied. "Do you know her personally?"

"No, no ... just some common friends..."

"So what's the problem, Mr. Bay?"

"My daughter is missing. Since, since Monday morning."

"Since yesterday, you mean."

"Right."

"How old is she?"

"Sixteen."

Delancey nodded and kept silent for a while. Then, he sighed, and said: "Mr. Bay, I'm the head of what my colleagues call the morgue squad. Do you know why? I deal with the most violent, psychologically impaired criminals, who inflict unspeakable pain on their neighbors. I do that work, because, well, not many things really affect me, you see? I don't have much in terms of sympathy or, what, fragility, or sensitivity. Right now I'm dealing with a case of two men brutally playing with and murdering a family with a five-year-old child. Now, you seem like a well-to-do man, and I'm sure you know a lot of other well-to-do men, influential people, so when one of you has a problem, it's just a matter of a friendly call to the head of the largest crime fighting organization in the country. But now tell me, Mr. Bay, is this office really the most well-suited place for a case of a rich teenage girl who didn't come home for a night? Wouldn't you say that's more of the ... the regular police matter? Or is calling the regular police beneath you?"

The plea in Francis' eyes turned to anger during Delancey's speech. Finally, he had a chance to answer.

"Have you finished, Agent Delancey? Fantastic. Because now I have something to say. I'm not the rich idiot you think I am. I've heard about teenagers sneaking out for a night. I'm raising Andrea on my own since her mother died when she was two. Okay? And it's not like that. What, you think I didn't call the police? They just do nothing. It's something else, Agent Delancey. Something very strange."

"Your contacts are enough to get me fired, Mr. Bay, so please continue. What's so strange?"

"It all started with our front door just getting knocked down. Saturday night, bam, it was down. No explanation. The next day, Andrea started to behave strangely. She slept the whole day. At night she came to me to say she's afraid of something. I have security cameras installed in my house, so I turned them on and went to work on Monday. But when I checked them from my office, all they showed was this."

Francis opened an app on his phone and showed it to Delancey. The rock over the ocean.

"It's what a camera at your house is showing?" Delancey asked. "You live on the shore?"

"As far from it as possible in Los Maines, Agent Delancey. We live in Lakoff."

"Lakoff!"

Francis noticed the surprise in Delancey's voice.

"Yes. Why?"

Because that's where the two men in white murdered the family on Sunday, thought Delancey, but he didn't say anything.

"It's a current feed," Francis continued. "That's what all cameras installed in my house are showing since she went missing. But when I checked the recordings, this is what I found."

Delancey stared at Francis as he fumbled with the app's controls with his trembling fingers.

"This is Monday," he said. "The terrace camera. Ten twenty-three."

On the screen, Delancey saw a well-trimmed lawn, and on the left side, in mid-distance, a teenage, brown-haired girl lying on a hammock, covered with a blanket, apparently sleeping.

"Now..." Francis said.

The girl lifted her head and stared to the right of the screen, her brow furrowed, her face attentive and surprised. She stayed in that position for a few seconds, then she got out of the hammock and disappeared into the bushes.

At that moment there was some interference in the recording; the vision garbled, some digital snow, and the familiar image of the rock over ocean waves filled the screen.

"I found her phone on the ground," Francis said. "There's a seven-foot wall back there. My housekeeper was in the front. Didn't see anyone leaving nor coming."

"Your girl's saying something before going there," Delancey said. "There's no sound?"

"No ... but, she's saying something? How do you know?"

"Well, I have eyes. Rewind it. Can you zoom?"

Andrea's pixelated face filled the screen as she lifted her head from the pillow and looked to the back of the yard. It was hard to notice, but she did start speaking before turning her head, and for a moment her lips were visible—

Delancey read her lips: "'Who are you?'"

The ocean waves filled the screen.

The two men looked at each other.

"Andrew, the boy—" Beatrice stood in the door, and as soon as she started speaking, Gabriel came from behind her into the office and looked at Francis with surprise.

"Oh, you're, you're Andrea's friend from school, aren't you?" Francis said, and turned to Delancey. "What is he—?"

"He's an important witness in our current investigation," Delancey said. "In fact, I think it's best he comes with us."

Francis was elated. "You're going to see what happened with my daughter?"

"Isn't that what you wanted, Mr. Bay?"

· · ·

"An important witness?" Beatrice said as they walked through the garage to her car.

"What was I supposed to tell him? That he's our magic boy clairvoyant who solves cases for us?"

"Point taken."

Beatrice opened her car.

"We go in the back seat," Delancey said to Gabriel.

As they drove up the ramp out to the street, he leaned down on his knees.

"Down!" he said to Gabriel. "Don't ask."

"What...?"

"I said don't ask! Get down now."

Gabriel lowered himself.

Beatrice pulled into the street, where Francis' elegant black SUV waited. They followed it.

"Why are we doing this?" Gabriel asked.

Delancey straightened himself and took a cautionary look behind.

"There. The blue sedan parked by the kiosk. See it?"

"What about it?"

"Crowe's men. CAISA. You did a very stupid thing coming to my office. I don't know how you entered the building..."

"I told the garage door to let me in and took the elevator."

"Don't ever do that again. What they want is you, and they suspect I know where you are. You coming to my office just like that is ... damn irresponsible."

"I can deal with humans," said Gabriel curtly, looking through the window.

They followed Francis's SUV through the traffic.

"You think the girl going missing is connected to those 'Princes?'" Beatrice asked.

"Well..." Delancey shrugged. "It happened five-hundred-yards away from the Dowleys' property. On the next day after the killing. And it does sound weird as hell."

"I came here because I have a favor to ask," Gabriel said to Delancey.

"You could've called. I check my phone for spyware daily, so it would be at least safe from those hounds. What do you want?"

"You have access to people's personal files, right?"

"What do you mean?"

"Well, like everybody's job and address and, like, police records..."

"Okay. And what you're getting at?"

"I want you to see what you can find about my father."

Delancey's stare softened.

"What's his name?"

"Michael West."

THE BAYS LIVED in the older, more elegant section of Lakoff. No identical suburban houses, only villas, swimming pools, and large, lush yards.

They followed Francis through the wooden gate in the wall surrounding his property. It was interesting for Gabriel to see how Andrea lived. He'd never been here of course. He'd never had courage to ask her out or just talk with her about anything more than classes and homework.

Her home was modern and expensive, with lots of dark wood and glass, something you only saw in TV shows about well-to-do people. They went around the house to the huge back yard, where the terrace floor was covered with wood, with a real Jacuzzi built in, next to a small kidney-shaped swimming pool. Then there was grass, some flowerbeds, a stone grill, picnic table, and the hammock.

"Bea," Delancey said, "could you please check the surveillance system? And log on to the cameras to see why the hell they show water instead of the back yard. I'll have a look around the place."

She nodded. Francis was still surprised with Gabriel's presence, but didn't say anything.

"Here, follow me," he said, and led Beatrice inside.

"Well? Let's see what we can see," Delancey said, and walked up with Gabriel to the hammock.

"Come out," Gabriel said.

The demon of the hammock was a southerner, a young man with a dreamy smile and beads in his dreadlocks.

"Chill and relax," he said. "Let's spend this lazy afternoon relaxing and dreaming. Why are you so tense, Ombudsman dude? Serious things, oh, serious things, needless tension and butthurt, who needs them?"

Gabriel made the Sign. "Tell me what happened on Monday."

"Sweet nothing, dude. The girl was resting. Then, she stood up and went. Day like every day."

"Where did she go?"

The Hammock lowered his eyes. Some of his chill seemed to have deserted him.

"Well, into the ... to the back of the yard."

"Why would she go there?"

"You know people! They always get some ideas, can't rest in peace, there's always some chore to do."

"She went to the back of the yard to work?"

"I have no idea! She was here, and then she wasn't. She heard something I didn't hear and went to check it out. Now hop on, let's relax in the shadow. It's a perfect time for a small nap."

Gabriel looked at Delancey and shook his head.

"Just says she went to the back of the yard."

"Let's see over there."

They approached the green wall of the bushes. There was an opening and they pushed through the branches into the shadow. The shrubs spread on for several feet and there was the wall.

"Wall, come out. Did anyone cross you on Monday or ... well, at any time?"

The Wall was a burly man with a shaved head and a black security uniform.

"I would like to see them try!" he bellowed. "Nobody scales me. Maybe with a ladder, I guess. But who carries a ladder with them? Maybe a squirrel can get through, or, say, a cat, if it jumps from a tree. No other way. No, sir! I'm impenetrable. Two layers of fortified brick, a five-inch layer of concrete. There are bunkers weaker than me!"

"I'm impressed. So, did you maybe see Andrea come here on Monday morning?"

"Yeah, I did see the chick," the Wall nodded. "Want to know my judgement? She was stoned. Had those swimming eyes, like junkies, right? And walked like a sleepwalker. She went into the bush over there. And I didn't see her come out."

Gabriel pushed through the branches of the bush the Wall pointed at. There was nothing, just wet ground, and some pale mushrooms in a semi-circle.

"Was anyone else here?" Gabriel asked.

"Well, her father, the master of the house, came here like an hour later. He called her. 'Andrea, Andrea!' you know. And then he picked up something from the ground. And left running back to the house. In the evening, some cops came, they searched the whole yard, but found zilch, nada, nothing, and nobody— because who could they find with an impenetrable wall all around the property?"

"And nobody else was here? No two men in white clothes, with long hair?"

"You mean, like in a circus?"

"Circus? No, not really..."

"Moot point. I saw only her and the master of the house."

Gabriel thanked the demon and said it could go back into its totem.

"Andrea's father found something here," Gabriel told Delancey.

"Yes. Her phone."

"Let's take a look at it."

THEY CAME INSIDE through the terrace door into the low-key, comfortable living room. Claudine took them to Francis and Beatrice, who were checking the security panel in the garage. The screen showed the image of the tall rock over the ocean.

"It's ridiculous," she said. "Everything should work. I have no idea why it shows the sea."

"It's been hacked?"

"Well, someone could maybe intercept the feed, but not insert their own. This is a simple system. The video from cameras goes straight in here!"

She flicked through the selector of cameras. *Click, click, click.* Ocean, ocean, ocean. From slightly different angles.

Gabriel moved closer to the screen. He could swear he recognized something about the rock the cameras were showing, but he couldn't remember what it was.

"Francis, could you leave us?" Delancey asked.

"Excuse me?"

"I know we're in your home, but you asked us to help you find Andrea. So now I'm asking you to leave us here for a second. We have some confidential procedures."

"Oh." Francis had to think about it for a second. "Of course. Yes. If it helps find her..."

He walked out of the garage.

"Ask the system," Delancey told Gabriel.

Gabriel nodded and pointed at the control panel.

"Come out."

The demon of the surveillance system appeared before him, a woman in a silver uniform, and he immediately noticed something was wrong. She smiled at him and stared straight into his face with startlingly blue eyes.

"Hello? Demon? What's going on here? What's that image you're showing?"

The System didn't answer. Just smiled at him.

Gabriel felt his heart beat faster. Something was very wrong with the demon.

He looked around the garage and saw a camera in the corner of the ceiling. He pointed at it.

"Camera! Come out."

It was a small, balding man, smiling at him and staring with the same clear blue eyes.

"Maurice?" Gabriel said, feeling a shiver creep up his spine.

"Yes," the demon's calm voice answered, and Maurice appeared next to him, looking around the room with attention.

"What's up with them? They don't react. They just smile ... and don't look right,"

Maurice kept silent for a while.

"They seem ... possessed," he said finally. "They're not themselves."

"Possessed? By whom?"

Maurice sighed helplessly.

"I don't know, Gabriel. It's the first time I've seen something like that."

"Her phone!" Gabriel said.

"I have it," Beatrice answered calmly, and showed Andrea's phone in her hand. "From her father."

The demon of Andrea's phone, a sporty girl, had much better clothes than Li, not so trashy, and looked like a pop star. It was a much newer model after all. Her eyes were normal and she didn't seem so weird like the demons of the camera and surveillance system.

"Hi there!" she said with a wide smile and made the V sign with her fingers. "How are you, gang?"

"Gang..." Maurice, a rugged demon of an inner-city playground, repeated with a slightly bemused smile. "Now that's entertaining."

"You were with Andrea, your owner, on Monday morning," Gabriel said. "You were with her when she went to the back of the yard and disappeared."

Andrea's Smartphone's smile faded. A shadow flitted across her high-cheekbone face.

"What? No ... I don't know what you're talking about," she tried to lie with a nervous giggle. "Oops. Excuse me. I think I don't remember."

"I think you remember," Gabriel said, and made the Sign. "Tell me. Now."

The Smartphone began breathing hysterically; her eyebrows rose up in terror. Lowering her voice, she whispered:

"The shadows took her."

9

HOUSE OF STRONG MEN

"Shadows took her," Delancey repeated an hour later. "Not exactly something I can tell a worried father."

Gabriel didn't reply. He gobbled up his club sandwich with turkey, egg, bacon, and salad.

They sat in the booth of a diner at Old Lakoff's small square with its posh expensive grocers, jewelers, and free-trade coffee shops where the local suburban youth hung out when there was no time to go for the really exciting fun in the city. The diner was in the old-fashioned American style, a metal trailer with red leather seats and choice of burgers, steaks, and chicken wings.

"Yep, too many shadows in this work recently," Beatrice agreed, and washed down a bit of her steak with Coke. "If I'd known in time, I'd have gone to Hogwarts instead of the police academy."

Gabriel took a look at his phone and checked the time.

"Listen, I want to get back to the orphanage," he said. "I should be there keeping an eye on Matt. Not here stuffing myself."

"Andrew, actually you should stuff yourself some," Beatrice said, pointing with her fork at Delancey's table. He hadn't even touched his steak; he hovered over his plate, pale, his hair sticky with sweat on his forehead, downing black coffee one mug after another.

"So what do you think?" he changed the subject. "Weird case, but doesn't seem connected with the murder. We have to prioritize. Search for those, how you called them, 'Princes,' and leave the girl to the cops. Or wizards."

Gabriel frowned. He thought back to the times when his eyes would steal to Andrea sitting next to him in class, or running across their sports track in sweatpants and half-top, with her tumultuous chestnut-brown hair tied in a ponytail. He felt a sudden anger at the memory, burning in his heart. He was refused everything every other boy had. He always had to care and protect others. *Let her go missing*, he thought, clenching his jaw. *What do I care, she would never understand me anyway, with her Jacuzzis and house servants.*

"You're wrong," he said.

"Oh yeah?" Delancey raised one eyebrow and gave him a crooked smile. "Okay?"

"It is connected. I'm the link. I went to school with her. The killers destroyed my apartment. They murdered a kid who was kidnapped along with my brother. It all connects with me."

"There's the link, but I can't see what's the meaning behind it," Delancey said. "We just got to prioritize. Right?"

"I know. And that's what I'm doing as well." He stood up. "Are you going to drop me off at your office? I left my car there. I need to go and guard the orphanage."

"I GOT a call from a place I don't like to get calls from, Andrew," said Melissa Tornatore in the slow, disgusted tone she always seemed to take on while talking to her subordinates.

Delancey stood in the same office where Director Boleani took his life not so long ago. The carpet was different. Apparently blood and brains weren't so easy to wash off, or from what he knew about the budget-conscious provisions department, they would have done just that. The new director had the desk changed as well, to a modern, metal rectangle, not out of place on the starship *Enterprise*. Only the lamp above was the same, along with the feeling in his gut that he would always get while standing in this room: the impatience combined with humiliation.

He looked at Melissa Tornatore. The new director was a strongly built fifty-something woman with cascades of blond curls, which Beatrice suspected to be a wig, falling over the shoulders of her two-piece dresses, of which she had a seemingly endless supply. She looked like a TV celebrity past her prime. But those feminine attributes didn't make her wrinkled face and steely eyes any warmer.

"It was a call from the president's office," she continued.

Delancey forced a smile. "You're going golfing together?"

"Your humor..." Melissa frowned. "I don't like employees cracking jokes when I have something serious to say. Or do you think you're allowed to make snide comments because I'm a woman and not fit to be your superior?"

Delancey sighed. "No. I'm a great friend to women," he murmured.

"So you should be," Melissa said. "You should remember that for me to sit in this chair it took ten times the effort it takes a man. That should tell you about the fortitude of my character. And convince you to take me seriously."

"I'm sorry," Delancey said plainly. "It was just a joke. Did the president want to know about the investigation?"

"You would think," she said with anger. "You would think he was interested in that. But no. I got a slap on the wrist for you not cooperating with CAISA the other day."

Fucking Crowe, Delancey thought.

"I don't care for CAISA's shady business, and I don't care for people from outside telling me what to do," she said. "But that's not your call. You're not me, Delancey. When a CAISA agent tells you jump, you jump. Or else I pay for your insubordination."

"I just ... I wanted to take the little West boy to a safe house. I told you."

"I know. That's not what it's about. It's about his older brother."

"Okay."

"Do you know where Gabriel West is?"

"No, Director."

She laughed.

"That's what I told CAISA. I knew you wouldn't tell me even if you did. You're a ballsy character. But what I need to tell you in my role as your boss is that if you come across that information you are to inform CAISA immediately. And if they—or I—discover you're lying, and you are seeing him, or, say, taking him along with you to crime scenes, there will be a price to pay. Understood?"

They stood there, staring each other in the eyes, a ratty, disheveled agent and his strong, proud woman boss.

And then they both got the message on their phones and looked to check.

Another murder.

A MYSTERIOUS DEATH in one of the LM Deportivo gyms in the business district, the report said. Two men in white involved. Delancey drove there with Beatrice.

The gym lobby was full of hipsters in tank-tops and Instagram starlets in hot pants, a few strongmen whispering among themselves. Pump-up music still blared from the speakers; apparently nobody had thought of switching it off. Delancey, who frequented only a one-room, sweat-permeated gym in a basement of an apartment house in Ursenev, where he did several sets of deadlifts and bench presses with an old, scratched barbell, looked with interest at the shiny machines, water fountains, and wall screens showing motivational videos full of cross fitters' abs and speedbikers' butts.

The manager was a bulky guy with a crew-cut who looked like he had switched out a tracksuit for a suit only recently, and with him was an even bulkier, freckled redhead in a tank-top, evidently on steroids—he kept swallowing nervously, his Adam's apple jumping up and down.

"Jan Robkowski," the manager introduced himself to Delancey. "This is Ken. He's the instructor who was taking care of the gym when the ... incident ... happened." He nodded at the large guy in the tank-top.

"Wow, more cops," Ken muttered under his breath, and took Delancey from the lobby to the large, two-floored gym.

It was completely empty now, the machines, the free weight stations, the cardio section, save for several grim cops, who nodded at Delancey. Through the glass walls he could see the neighboring office towers full of corporation managers and assistants, busy at work at their desks.

"Agent," one of the cops greeted him, and led them to the machines section.

It took Delancey a while to actually understand what he was seeing. He just knew it was some sort of a machine, and a human body was somehow trapped in it, smashed and twisted in an unnatural manner, with the head low between the knees. Bile and blood had splashed on the floor.

"Careful you don't step in that," muttered the cop.

"So, what's the story behind this sad scene?" Delancey asked.

"According to the jock over there, two men came here around 11:30. Said they wanted to look around, taking advantage of the free trial offer. He sent them over to the locker room to change, but apparently they didn't. We have to take his word for it, as the cameras don't work."

"Of course."

"According to one of the girls from the nearby treadmill, the strangers went over to the victim and started talking to him. She heard they had an argument. The victim kept repeating 'I don't know, I don't know.' She said she felt threatened by the situation, and wanted to go and call somebody from the staff, but before she decided to do so, the two men left. And our victim, well, stayed. Apparently caught in the machine." The policemen patted the metal apparatus. "You know what that is, Agent?"

"Nah."

"It's an 'ab crunch' machine. Pushes you from behind, and you push back. It seems something went wrong and it pushed too hard. He couldn't call for help because, you see, he had no air left in his lungs anymore to do so. The machine went on pushing and crushing him to the state you see right now."

"Do we have an ID?"

"This was in his jacket."

Delancey knew the face and the name on the ID. He swore and shook his head.

"Agent?"

"Nothing. And the men?"

"And the men left, as I said." The cop shrugged. "Unperturbed. The instructor on duty swears he was out at the moment, because he had to do some cleaning in the locker room, but you know, I think he was just on his phone the whole time."

Delancey nodded.

"Thank you, Officer."

He went back to the reception.

"Please, Agent ... can I tell the clients it wasn't the faulty machine?" the manager pleaded, catching his elbow. "It was those two guys, right? The machines are great. DenX, it could never happen without tampering. I have to tell my clients something..."

"Tell your clients it's online yoga day today."

The manager frowned, nodded, and turned away.

"Wait," Delancey said. "So what's the story? I come in from the street, say I want the free trial, and you let me in? Without checking who I am?"

"Of course not. You have to fill out a form and give us all your personal data. Ken?"

The instructor shrugged with his large shoulders.

"Of course, boss."

"So, the two guys who talked with the victim, you have their personal info?" Delancey asked. "Let's see it."

Ken went to the counter and the bulbous muscles on his arms pulsed as he reached into the tray on his desk. He found two sheets of paper and stared at them with a frown. Delancey took the papers from his hands.

"Client name: Ninky Nonk," he read. "Address: Fairyland. The 'Personal ID type and number' isn't filled out. Let's see your second form. Ah, the name here is Pinky Ponk. Address, it says, 'In your head.'" He looked up at the very unhappy instructor. "What do you think? We have them?"

Ken didn't answer. He stared glumly at the floor.

"You didn't even look at what they put here. They came in, you were on your phone, gossiping or posting selfies with no shirt on, and you said sure, took the forms back and put them in this pretty tray here without even checking, and went back to your phone, ignoring or even not noticing that the feed from the cameras was gone. Am I very wrong here?"

"You have no proof what I did."

"I have no proof because the two fucks you let in here switched off the security cameras, Einstein. Whatever. I wasted enough time on you."

He went outside and saw Beatrice waiting for him at a table outside a coffeehouse, speaking on her phone, taking in reports from other divisions. He sat next to her and sipped some of her latte and grimaced at the syrupy sweetness.

She frowned and gave him a soft slap on his hand.

"Okay." She put away her phone. "Who was that?"

"One of Ruslan's men. Maxim. Was with us at the airport and at New Eden."

"Shit."

"You know what that means, don't you?"

"What?" she said.

"What do you mean, what? He was a part of the task force at Boleani's."

"That means..."

"There's a pattern and we're sitting on our asses in the dead middle of it. All of us can expect a visit, sooner or later."

They looked at each other.

"Have Oscar and Pete notify everybody connected to the Boleani case they're in danger," he said finally. "You too, don't go anywhere unarmed."

"And Gabriel?" Beatrice said.

"What about him?" he asked impatiently.

"We need to protect him, too."

He smiled. "You know the kid, he just wants to guard his brother."

"Yeah, but ... maybe we can lock them up somewhere..."

He thought for a while.

"Beatrice," he said eventually with resignation in his voice. "I have no idea if I can do a better job at protecting him than he can himself."

With sudden desperation, he realized how helpless and worthless he was against the two monsters on the prowl in his city. *Pathetic.*

"What more can we do?" he growled, and slammed his fist on the table. Patrons looked at him with sour faces. "We posted the facial composite online, but who follows our damn social media feeds? Every halfwit taking photos of their own butt with a selfie stick has more followers than us and the police combined. We got them on the news, but who watches the news? Old, retired mummies who don't leave home anyway and who forget what they saw before they go back from the kitchen with their cookies. What can we do, Bea? Buy ads on YouTube? Lock everybody at home? Well, it so happens they can get you at home. Lock everybody in one damn bunker?"

"We can put wanted posters at subway and bus stops," she pointed out.

"You're right. That's actually a good idea. Tell Pete to do that. I want to see their ugly mugs each step I take in this damn city."

He grimaced. Brain zaps, like small electric shocks inside his head, he was getting them more and more often. Always accompanied by a long, biting pain, and a feeling of incoming doom—Atroposine withdrawal symptoms.

"Do you want me to drive you home?" she asked.

He shook his head.

"I'm sleeping at the firm until we solve it," he said.

10

THE MEADOW OF DREAMS

ANDREA OPENED her eyes and didn't understand where she was and what was happening to her. She felt like ages had passed in some hypnotic slumber since the time she lay in the hammock in their backyard. Now she was somewhere else. Her eyelids were heavy with sleep and her limbs were slow and lazy, like trapped in slowly hardening liquid amber. All she saw was a dark purple dome above her, with vertical slits—narrow openings, like those between heavy curtains, through which a breeze came and she thought she could see fragments of the night sky and shining stars. The whole world undulated slowly and she could hear a slow song, so quiet on the verge of hearing, and so beautiful, like a long-forgotten melody, that it made her heart cry in remembrance of distant years when she was a child and the world was magic.

She stared up for some time, feeling as if she'd returned home after many years of wandering, and then, slowly, what she thought was a dome above her began unfolding: an opening appeared in the middle, at the very top, and grew wider and wider as what she thought were curtains parted, revealing the night sky full of stars so many she never could see above the light-polluting city.

This awakened her from another waft of sleep that had tried to overcome her, and she sat up, determined to find out where she was.

She saw she was completely naked and sitting on something like a round, yellow and furry bed, some seven feet in diameter.

The purple curtains rose from the floor all the way up, surrounding the bed without so much as a trace of a door or any other way of exit.

She stood up on the soft floor, and her abode moved slightly as she tilted her weight, and she quickly crouched and leaned herself on her hands to prevent further motion. A stupefying suspicion appeared in her mind. She took one more look around her and suddenly she was certain.

She was inside a giant, tulip-like flower.

It seemed natural, even though that was, of course, impossible. What she took for a bed felt natural and fleshy to the touch; it wasn't fur, it was made of hundreds of yellow carpels, like the disc inside a daisy, or a chamomile. It couldn't have been an artificial material. And the smell permeating the air was sweet and heavy. She realized she had smelled that scent for an inordinate amount of time; it had permeated her dreams as she lay unconscious, submersed in unrecognizable visions.

But how was that possible? There were no flowers the size of a bungalow. Slowly, one by one, memories started to appear. Their front door, broken by an unseen force. The voices from the bushes in the back yard. The callings. Her transformation.

On all fours, to keep her balance in case the flower tilted, Andrea crawled up to the giant petals. She slid her hands between them; they were soft and meaty, like velvet, and she pushed them apart.

She saw a meadow at night, stretching far, far away, to a dark wall of a forest on the horizon. The meadow was full of tall grass and flowers, moving softly in the warm wind, and even though the sky was black and full of stars, somehow everything was visible. There were little wavering lights, like fireflies maybe, scuttling about, flying from flower to flower. Over the distant forest, strange lightning would appear on the horizon, completely silent and thunder-less, as if some faraway, eternal but peaceful thunderstorm raged on beyond the border of the world.

She looked down and her head spun. She was well over fifty feet above the ground, and the only way down seemed to be the flower stem. Either she had shrunk very, very small, or it was a land of giants. But that thought didn't move her as much as it would in a normal life.

Then she fell on her back as a strange being flew into the flower she was in. She covered her womb and chest and stared with awe at the intruder.

It was a little man, naked but also lacking any kind of body features associated with sex; the person was quite round, with big eyes and a very wide mouth. He had a pair of wings growing from his back and seemed to emit a golden glow.

"Who are you?" Andrea whispered.

"I'm sorry," the creature said softly. "I'm just looking for a place to die. I thought this place was empty."

"But ... who are you?"

"Well ... I am me," the creature answered.

"What is this place? What am I doing here?"

"Oh. Yes. You. You are our treasure. I'm sorry for disrupting your rest. I will die any moment now and I need to find a place for myself. Excuse me, Eden. I have to go. Someone will take you to him shortly."

"Eden?"

But the creature slipped through the giant petals and flew away.

Andrea sat down on the soft disc to try to understand what was happening. She felt another wave of oblivion overtake her body; she wavered and fell back and closed her eyes and drifted off to sleep.

What awoke her was a loud buzzing outside. One of the petal walls vibrated. She stood up and waited a second to see what would happen.

"Hello?" she said, but there was no answer.

Carefully, ready to jump back at any moment, she moved the petals apart and looked out. There was a huge bee, the size of a horse, hanging in the air in front of her, flapping its wings so fast her hair waved in the breeze.

She stared at the hairy insect with wide open eyes.

"What do you want?" she said finally.

The bee flapped its wings and made a turn in the air so that it was slightly below the bloom, easy for her to step down, and she understood she was supposed to mount it.

"No. No, no, no, not a good idea," she said, but the bee just buzzed louder and pushed her softly with its striped fuzzy belly.

"I'm not flying on you. Okay?" Andrea said, but then she heard a voice booming from far away. The voice called: "Eden!" and she knew it was her it called. It grew darker and colder all around, as if in response to the emotions of the owner of the voice, as if the world were one living being.

And she knew she had to obey.

She sighed, whispered: "Here goes nothing," and jumped onto the bee with wide open arms.

The hair covering the bee's body was stiff and pointy, and scratched her naked skin. It vibrated under her, as if she sat on a running dishwasher.

The bee soared, carrying her in a dizzying flight over the meadow. They passed the tall blades of grass and flowers and wandering lights and Andrea found herself laughing in amazement. It was miles beyond any trip you could ever imagine under the influence of exotic substances in the corner of dark room at a sophomore party. It was real and it was amazing.

They flew through a wall of trees and it got darker and

colder. The bee lowered her flight and sat on a branch which was like a huge, fallen tree to Andrea.

"Are we there?" she asked. The bee sat patiently, so she slid off it and stood on the wood. At the very moment, the bee took flight and Andrea ducked, afraid of its sudden movement.

The bee flew away.

Covering her private parts, Andrea looked around.

She stood on a large bough lodged into the grassy shore of a pond of black water that reflected the starry sky above like a perfect, clear mirror. All around the pond was the dark forest, its trees high like tower blocks of her city. One weeping willow on the shore dipped its long leaves in the water. There were lily pads floating on the pond and giant toads sitting on them. Now and then a toad would jump in the air and catch one of the phosphorescent flies with its long sticky tongue, and splash into the water.

Again, Andrea heard the bird with the almost human voice, like on that distant night of the break-in, the bird calling something among the forest, like speaking a spell, and then a gigantic shape covered half the sky. She could guess its contours only by the obscuration of the stars: it was like a demigod, giant, covered with tangled hair, with a set of wide horns on its massive head.

The giant spoke to her in its low, booming voice, calmly, as if it had eons of immortal patience: "We were waiting for you, Eden."

"I'm Andrea," she answered.

The being shifted its head. "That was your name, yes. It was ugly. Now you have a name that is beautiful. You are Eden, the Watcher on the Rock."

"What do you want from me?"

"We want you to protect us, Eden. You will save our lives and you will kill our enemies."

"But ... who are you?"

"We are the world, Eden. What was long before you came.

We are the grass that covers your fallen temples. We are the spirits of life. And I will give you command over the spirits of life so you can save us from the human and his book, and from the Rising Star."

"I don't understand."

"You will bring down the Rising Star and you will kill Ombudsmen who bring chaos into the eternal order—you will end the suicidal reign of men."

"What is the Rising Star? And Ombudsmen?"

"See for yourself."

And in a terrible vision Andrea saw the Earth scorched, humans covered with ash, their skin burned, as they crawled through the smoking wasteland howling for a drop of water and an inch of shade. Terrible pain exploded in her heart and she broke down weeping, as if she felt the pain of the whole of creation dying a cosmic death and dissolving into nothing. It was a vision that blazed a mark on her soul, a pain she knew she could never forget.

"Do you understand me now, Eden?" the god asked, and she found herself nodding, tears streaming down her cheeks, her mouth open in wordless weeping. "You must do everything in your power to not let it come to pass."

"Yes, yes," she sobbed.

"Then go, sweet child, rest and gather strength ... and awake when you are ready for the great deeds. I will show you the place of your watch. And remember this word: *Ahanari*. In your name, spirits will kill. *Ahanari*."

The shadow rose until it covered the whole of the sky and she had to kneel down, overtaken by weakness. Then she fell face down onto the giant bough, sleeping and gathering strength.

.   .   .

Wearing a red tracksuit and listening to an energetic track on her headphones, twenty-seven year-old Elisa Nimkin ran through the forest on the edge of Lakoff District. Her dog, a great Dane, ran next to her, happy and panting with his tongue hanging out.

She'd chosen a different route today, and was starting to fear that she was lost: the undergrowth got taller and she kept tripping over the roots of thick trees, whose canopies obscured the sunlight.

Her dog caught some irresistible scent: he lay his ears along his head and lifted his black, sniffing snout, and after a moment of tension he darted into the bushes. She could only hear his barking and cracking of the branches.

"Brutus! Damn you!" she cried "Brutus!"

More barking. This time it sounded desperate ... and afraid?

She looked around and found a thick branch on the ground. She followed her dog slowly and carefully. Now she was really sorry she didn't choose her usual jogging route.

She pushed through a thorny shrubbery and lost her breath at what she saw.

There was a wide space between the trees, like a room with a ceiling of foliage, through which several rays of the sun fell in, drawing an intricate pattern of light. Small particles of shining dust floated in the air in a slow, mysterious dance.

On a bed of moss, surrounded with mushrooms and berries, lay a naked girl with long, chestnut hair. A snail traversed her thigh. A jay sat on her head and stared at Elisa like she was an intruder. A squirrel sat at the girl's feet, with a round nut in its tiny paws. And Elisa's dog hunched low to the ground, growling with menace, his hair all standing and making him look like a porcupine. He stared with fearful rage into the bushes. She looked there and saw a huge fat snout and two tusks, and realized a wild boar was among the forest animals surrounding the naked girl.

Elisa noticed all that in a fraction of a second, turned on her heels and ran back towards civilization, checking behind her for the wild boar. But fortunately only her dog followed in her footsteps.

As soon as she could see a street outside the forest, she bent in half and vomited. Then, she sat on a fallen log, crying hysterically. The dog came up to her, nervous with his owner's emotion, and licked her face, trying to help.

She pushed him away and reached for a phone and quickly dialed three digits.

"I need police, or an ambulance, or something," she said. "There's a dead body in the forest. I found a dead body in the forest."

FRANCIS WALKED down the white corridor, pushing through the nurses and patients in hospital gowns.

"Hey, you! Watch your step!" someone yelled at him, but he didn't react. With determination on his face, he pressed ahead. The cellphone in his pocket kept ringing.

He reached for it and looked at the screen—Alek, his boss, the CEO of Maxravel.

"I've no time!" he snapped into the phone. "I told you. They found my daughter!"

He found the room number he looked for and pulled open the door.

Inside there was a small, bald man in a white coat.

"Mr. Bay?" the doctor said. "I think we talked. Doctor Carl Antracy."

Francis stepped into the room and looked at the bed.

There she was, his daughter, covered with a white sheet, her face pale and unscathed, with only a small narrow cut on her right temple, which continued down to the middle of her cheek.

Her hair was undone, forming an aura around her head. She was very pale.

"How is she?" he whispered.

"Mr. Bay..." Doctor Carl said. "This is a coma room. I understand you know what that means."

"She's asleep."

"Not exactly. At a moment of intense stress, our mind can switch off, so to speak, to recuperate, and prevent further damage. "

"Can you ... wake her up?"

"Knowing when the brain switches back on, and if it does so at all, is sadly beyond the reach of today's medicine. Some people wake up after years, some ... don't."

Francis felt tears welling in his eyes.

"Listen," he said. "I don't care about the cost. If there is any ... medicine, any form of therapy you can try..."

The bald doctor gave him a sad smile.

"Of course there is. There's acupuncture, verticalization, hydrotherapy, even dogotherapy, if you desire. A man with your means will find countless gurus and experts selling you magic cures. Then you will become bound to this bed, staring at her face, interpreting every tic of her mouth, every involuntary grimace, as means of communication." He put a hand on Francis' shoulder. "It's a dead end, Mister Bay. They will promise you miracles. And here we don't deal with miracles. This is the field of medicine." Antracy reached under her bed and lifted a small plastic bag with yellow liquid.

"What's that?" Francis asked.

"It's a drainage bag, collecting your daughter's urine through a catheter. I show it to you so you understand straight away the realities of your situation. This is medicine, not hypnosis, music therapy, all those smokescreens. We make sure that she's healthy and she doesn't get bedsores ... and that's it. As a doctor, all I can recommend now with a pure conscience, is … just wait. Pray, if you have a faith. Or just put your trust in real medicine. There are fates worse than a coma."

Francis didn't find strength to answer. He just nodded.

The doctor gave him a reassuring smile, squeezed his arm, and left the room.

Francis sat on a small chair, trying to organize his thoughts.

He was overcome with joy when they found her. He was afraid of her new condition and full of worry for the future. But it was better than those terrible days, filled with dread. He couldn't sleep, but he had to remain sane, so he'd kept going to work, even though he couldn't understand what people said to him. And now it was over. Or was it just the beginning?

His daughter looked so calm. It was only afternoon, but he felt all the weariness accumulated through the sleepless nights, and dozed off in the little chair. At the verge of falling asleep, he took one last look at Andrea, and jumped up and cried in fear.

For a split second he saw a pulsating brown tumor, similar to a polypore, hovering in the air three feet above her chest. Some of its many long, twisted, appendages slipped under her covers, others connected to her aorta, others to her temples. The brown polypore pulsated, as if it was one brown and vascular beating heart.

He shut his eyes, opened them again, and it was gone. He was seeing things. He was too tired.

He crossed the room to a small bathroom and splashed his face with cold water.

Then he heard her saying something. He frowned and went back to the room.

She had a grimace on her face, as if in pain. She groaned and turned her head on the pillow rapidly.

"Why?" Andrea said, and listened to some inaudible reply. "Where? No. I want to stay here."

He leaned over her bed and listened, trying to hear her

better. But she stopped speaking and her forehead smoothed out.

"Andrea?" Francis whispered, close to her face.

She said a word he didn't understand at first. And when he did, he stood back in surprise.

"What did you say?" he said, but she didn't answer.

He went to the door.

"Nurse!" he cried into the corridor. "Nurse!"

11

MANHUNT

In the light, dripping rain, Delancey walked out of the house on Bildersman Avenue. He ducked under the police tape, crossed the yard to the fence, and leaned against it. Nausea gurgled in his stomach. He spat on the ground. One more time. He thought he would vomit, but he didn't. He looked up to the overcast sky and shook his head. Bastards.

He thought about calling Gabriel to come and interrogate the demons, but he found he really didn't want to bring him here. He wanted to spare him. Beatrice would cut off his balls if she found out.

A blackbird sat on the fence, tilting its feathered head with its eyes like two shiny marbles, and seemed to stare at Delancey. Somehow it didn't mind the rain. The agent winked at it.

"I'm getting soft," murmured Delancey to the bird, and scowled.

He returned to the crime scene. The cops were understanding enough not to ask him why he had left so suddenly.

The first victim was Officer Geoff Kinaski in his workshop in the garden shed. He was standing, but not on his own. His hand was attached to the workbench, with the electric drill still sticking from it, and his feet were nailed to the floor, the nail gun lying nearby. His whole body was strangely contorted, and Delancey saw why after he raised the victim's shirt with a ruler. His belt was pulled so tight that his body looked like an hourglass, the belt squeezing the contents of his stomach up through his mouth and nostrils, staining the man's chin and shirt.

Further on, the entryway of the house was totally black and porous, much like Gabriel had described his apartment.

Geoff's wife was in the kitchen, sitting on the tiled floor, with her head hanging back and her neck cut with a tightened necklace. Assessing her purple face and swollen tongue, he decided the cause of death was strangulation, although that was not everything. Only one leg stuck out of her skirt. The other leg was inside the still running oven she sat opposite.

"It looks bad, Bea," Delancey said into the phone. "It's fucking dark."

"What else is new?" she answered.

"Yeah. Nothing under the sun."

"Witnesses?"

"A neighbor saw them. Two guys in white, on a bike, leaving the crime scene at dawn, when he was out to get his milk. As they passed him, they shouted something he didn't quite catch, and then his lawnmower turned on by itself and rushed at him."

"Who are the victims?"

"Yeah, I don't know yet. Geoff Kinaski? Seems he was a uniform guy. There's some equipment like a gun, and pepper spray."

"Let me check."

He could hear her typing something into her computer, while he stared dumbly at the leg in the oven. Surreal.

"Okay," she said. "I got a match. Worked as security at Los Maines International Airport."

Delancey cursed.

"Boleani connection, again."

They went silent. A coroner entered the kitchen and

looked at Delancey with questions in her eyes. He nodded, allowing her to get on with collecting the bodies, and went outside again. It was good to feel the cool wind and drops of water on his face after the stuffy, warm insides of the house of death.

Delancey had to call a cab to the office. The blackbird still sat on the fence. He waved his hand. "Shoo!"

The bird flapped its wings and took to flight, spattering tiny drops of rain.

With his hood low over his eyes, Gabriel walked in the rain up and down the street on which the orphanage was located. He couldn't bear sitting in the old lady's apartment listening to its demons talk about her ungrateful grandsons, her numerous cats who had to be taken to a shelter after her demise, and her victories at old ladies' bridge tournaments. By observing the orphanage through the window, he learned by heart the hours in which the cops stationed there took their turns, what they ordered from local takeouts, what they looked like. He gave them names in his mind. From time to time, a strange man in a suit would go outside for a breather, and Gabriel knew they were the CAISA agents. The cops and agents never talked with each other, just stared at each other with hate.

From time to time, he would see a boy's silhouette in one of the orphanage's tall windows, and his heart would beat faster at the thought that maybe it was his little brother.

He felt like wild game waiting for hunters to come. It was unbearable.

Captain Nakamura did his discreet rounds between the orphanage roof and the apartment to charge up. As he had a good vantage point, he didn't have to fly for too long, so the charging sessions weren't frequent. It was an old people's district, with not many of them taking the exertion to raise their tired heads up to the sky, but the presence of spies and policemen posed a danger of being spotted.

Gabriel decided to go to a Chinese restaurant down the road for some takeout. It was tiny and full of impoverished workers from the area. He ordered chicken in coconut dough and rice. At the checkout, he told the cash register to not be very demanding on his debit card. The smiling girl at the register didn't understand any of what he said and that made it easier.

A lucky cat waved its paw at him from the back shelf.

As he left the restaurant, it stopped raining. He was on his way back when Li appeared.

"Incoming call from a strange number I don't know," he said. "Seems local."

"Okay," Gabriel reached into his pocket and answered the phone.

"Hello?"

"Gabriel...? This is Andrea's father."

"Oh ... hello, Mister Bay. Did you find her?"

"Actually, we did, yes."

"That's very good news! Is she okay?"

Francis sighed; there was some hesitation in his voice.

"She's ... sleeping, Gabriel. We're at St. Mary's Hospital on Minstral Avenue."

"Is she hurt? Unconscious?"

"She's not hurt. But listen, why I am calling is ... she said something strange in her sleep. Something that sounds a bit, well, how to say it ... immature?" He laughed uncomfortably. "Something I thought maybe her school friends would know the meaning of."

"What was it?" Gabriel stopped. What a strange call.

"Birdflipper."

"What?"

"She said that she doesn't want to go to the Birdflipper. Does that tell you anything?"

"To be honest, no. Well, you know what flipping the bird means, right?"

"The 'fuck you' gesture? Yes, of course. But I thought maybe you had some code at school and it meant something more ... that there was someone you called that..."

"I wasn't so close with your daughter, Mr. Bay. Maybe you should try her friend Mila?"

"Yes, I already did. She doesn't know either. There's one more thing, too."

"Yes?"

"She asked, 'What is Ombudsman?' Does that tell you anything, Gabe?"

Gabriel looked at Maurice, who appeared next to him with an astonished expression on his face. Gabriel shrugged at him.

"I'm sorry, Mr. Bay."

"Okay. Well. It was a long shot. Thank you." Andrea's father disconnected.

Gabriel stood there and stared in silence at Maurice.

"Why would she ask about an Ombudsman?" he said eventually.

"It's really strange," the demon agreed.

Gabriel shook his head.

"Okay. I have no mind space left to get into that. I think we're really unprepared and we have to work on it."

"Unprepared for what?"

"The attack."

Evening was coming. Gabriel returned to the old lady's apartment and sat at the table with his gun laid out in front of him. He cleaned and reloaded it.

"I'm good as new and ready for some wet work," hissed Alyssa, the demon of his gun, with pleasure. "Let me just see their ugly mugs. Bang! Bang! They're dead."

Gabriel stood up to see how fast he could draw the gun, and what place of concealment would be best. He decided on his hoodie's front pocket. It ran across his belly and there was a lot of space inside.

"Li," he said to the demon of his phone. "As soon as you see there's trouble, call Agent Delancey, Agent Beatrice, then just 911. First thing, tell them the location. Then, the nature of emergency."

"Understood," Li nodded his head.

"It's good to see you, Captain Nakamura," Gabriel said as the drone flew in through the window.

The captain bowed. "What are your plans for me?"

"Well ... reconnaissance, like now."

"But I can attack, too," Nakamura said. "I've heard of a man who attached an AK47 assault rifle to a Miksand Drone, and installed pneumatic triggers..."

"Yeah, well ... Captain, you're talking about a major mod here. I don't think we have time and tools for that. Or expertise."

"Oh," Captain Nakamura seemed disappointed he wasn't getting an onboard machine gun. "Here's a thought. A grenade. I could have a grenade, or an explosive attached. Would be easier to mount."

"I guess so, although getting my hands on a grenade could be problematic. But then, you would die in the attack."

"So?" Captain Nakamura answered, and Gabriel remembered the Japanese kamikaze, the divine wind, crashing into enemy ships in their suicide attacks.

"Here's the thing, Captain. You're much more use to me alive. And when it comes to fisticuffs ... you could always, like, ram into the attacker?"

Nakamura thought for a moment, then nodded.

"Will do," he said.

"Great. So, if you're charged, please go back to your patrol."

"Yes, Gabriel-San!"

The drone flew out the window and Gabriel looked at Maurice.

"I would look good on your wrist," said the demon. "And serve you with good advice."

Gabriel nodded and sighed.

"I'm tired of all this already. Go back into your totems."

The room went clean of all demons and he was alone in the old lady's apartment, smelling of mothballs and heart drops. He leaned on the window ledge and pressed his forehead against the glass. Behind the monumental building of the orphanage, the setting sun turned the low-hanging clouds to fire. It was the only moment during that ugly day that he saw any other color than gray.

Gabriel looked at the police cars, and black heavy government cars of the CAISA agents parked along the quiet street. He wondered how strong in battle they would prove against the unknown killers. Could they defend the children living there from two Ombudsmen with extended powers? For himself, he would be hesitant to attack anyone who was armed, even if theoretically he could gain control over the person's weapon. Commanding demons took time and didn't always work. Even though they were born to serve humans, they remained capricious, unpredictable entities.

Suddenly, he felt he couldn't bear another lonely evening in this apartment, staring at the gate and windows of the orphanage, his heart beating stronger with each car passing in the street below.

He had to get outside. And he realized he really wanted to see Andrea.

MEANWHILE, Delancey sat at his desk and went through traffic reports, looking for anything regarding the Ducate bike. In the corner of his office there was a folding bed with a pillow and blanket where he'd spent last night, and a suitcase with a change of clothes.

Beatrice walked quickly into his office, and it was enough for him to see her face to jump to his feet.

"We have them," she said. "Somebody recognized them from the posters."

THEY WERE SPEEDING down the main artery of the city. Delancey sat beside Beatrice, feeling the thrill of the hunt building up in his chest.

"We got a call from a French restaurant in the center," she told him. "A waiter recognized the Princes from the wanted posters. They're dressed in white and they're sitting deep inside the room, by the wall. Table twelve. But how the hell are we supposed to know which is table twelve?"

"Can we get Ruslan's team?"

"He's collecting his men and they're on their way. ETA, thirty minutes."

"Too long. Can't afford it. Get as many cops as you can. Tell the street patrols to cut off all roads leading to the restaurant.

"It's the center of the city—"

"Yeah, I don't give a goddamn. Are we in contact with the manager on site?"

"Yes. They just got their hors d'oeuvres."

"What the hell is that?"

"Appetizers, I think."

"Good. They won't like their dessert." Delancey took out his gun and reloaded it with a metallic clank.

They stopped at the curb before the crossing. On the other side they saw the restaurant on the corner, "*Champs Elysees.*" Delancey could see people eating inside, a posh bunch. Shiny chandeliers, cups of ice cream, dishes served under silver domes. The streets outside were already cut off by traffic patrols so no cars passed by. For a fraction of second he marveled at seeing the busy crossing so empty.

"Chief…" Pete and Oscar ran up to him from their SUV, breathless, holding their guns. He nodded at them and got out. They crouched behind Beatrice's car, where they could have a clear view of the restaurant, keeping contact with Beatrice through the open car door.

"Tell the manager they can serve the main meal in five. Or anytime earlier if the two seem impatient.'

"Roger that."

Delancey saw the first cops coming from the right of the restaurant, two women and three men, running close to the wall and stopping just before the main entrance. He waved at them and made a "stop and wait" sign.

"Is there a back door?" he asked Beatrice.

Beatrice listened to the answer from the manager.

"Through the kitchen. Exit's from the side of Tepicki Street," she repeated.

"Okay." Delancey licked his dry lips in excitement. He turned to Oscar: "Send the next patrol to guard the back exit. Go there with Pete. You'll help with evacuation."

"Yes, Chief." Oscar and Pete ran to the other side and dived into a dark alley.

Delancey saw the SWAT van roll in and stop on the left side of the crossing. One by one, armed SWAT operators ran across the road, where some took positions opposite the restaurant and aimed their rifles at the windows.

"Ruslan's here. Good."

His phone rang. He picked up.

"Ruslan?"

"Yeah, I'm in the van. A blind person could see you. Move back behind your car a little."

"Okay. They're two tall men, white suits. What do you got?"

"We got the floor plan of the restaurant with the tables."

"They're table twelve."

"Shit. It's in the opposite end. We have like five occupied tables before them. Do we wait for them to leave, or—"

"I think it's the only way, actually," Delancey said. "Too many people in there. I'll have them evacuate whoever they can, but not the patrons. Let them have their dinner in peace, and as they leave, and you have a clear mark, let your men just open fire. Just mow down the sons of the bitches. Don't waste time for any warnings, nothing."

"Yeah, I think you're right. Just move the damn cops away from the entrance."

"Got it."

"I think we'll take position close to the wall, actually," Ruslan continued, "and try to take them down from behind. Only snipers from the front. Headshots. I'm sending one up into the apartments above to see if he gets a visual from a window."

"Perfect."

Delancey disconnected and reached out to Beatrice in the car.

"Give me that, please."

He put on her earpiece.

"Hello, Senior Agent Delancey here. You're the manager on site?"

"Yes, yes..." a nervous woman's voice sounded in his ear. "They're eating and talking. Laughing."

"Okay, won't laugh for long. Listen ... take all kitchen crew and all personnel you don't need to serve them to the outside, through the back door—everybody you can evacuate without arousing their suspicion. That is, everybody who's not in the main room now."

"Got it."

"Now, for this you need the best actor you got among your waiters. Do the triage. Select one table where you have women or children. Let your waiter come up to them and tell them there is a situation, they should not react in any nervous way: they just need to leave now, without looking around, without talking, absolutely without running. Then, after three minutes, do the same with another table. Do that in three-minute intervals until I tell you that's enough."

There was silence as the only reply.

"Did you get that?" Delancey asked.

The response froze his blood: high-pitched, ridiculous laugher.

"Hello?" He tapped the earpiece and moved the microphone closer to his lips. "Are you there?"

"Just who are you and what the fuck are you playing at?" answered an amused, lisping voice in his earpiece, and he felt the hair stand up on the nape of his back.

"Who's there?" Delancey asked through a clenched throat.

And then—*BOOM!*—all the windows in the restaurant exploded and terrified screams filled the street.

"Go, go, go!" yelled Ruslan from the SWAT van, and his operators stormed the restaurant through the broken windows.

Beatrice and Delancey grabbed their guns and ran.

The inside of the restaurant was full of dust, patrons crawling on the floor, wounded and bloodied by glass, everyone screaming.

Gun in hand, Delancey scanned the crawling bodies for white clothes—he saw movement at the door in the back.

"The kitchen!" he shouted to Beatrice, and ran towards the door when a roaring flame exploded from the passage like a fiery paw, taking down the incoming SWAT operators; the kitchen was a burning inferno, a room filled with open fire, from the floor to the ceiling.

He heard gunshots outside.

"Back exit!" he cried, and ran out of the restaurant. A white motorbike dashed past him; the two were sitting on it, and they sped away down the road. Oscar and Pete ran out of the side street, shooting after the Princes.

"They fucking ran on the wall!" Pete yelled.

"To the cars! Follow them!" cried Delancey.

Beatrice jumped behind the wheel and he sat beside her. She started with screeching tires, chasing the motorbike. They could see it ahead. Delancey called the traffic division.

"They're approaching the barrier at Flote Street! Two men on a motorbike! Shoot them without warning!"

They were close to the barrier. He saw the police cruisers parked across the street, blocking it and the bike getting closer, and he heard gunshots.

"Cut off the sidewalk! Fuck's sake!" he roared into his phone as he saw an opening between a wall and a streetlight. One of the cops missed his shot and he saw a bullet hole in their windshield. "Hold fire, you'll kill us!"

The motorbike veered onto the sidewalk and dashed past the barrier. Beatrice stopped; the car was too wide to fit there.

"Move those damn cars!" yelled Delancey. "Follow them!"

The cops ran into their cruisers and began backing them up and turning into the lane. They drove down the street, sirens blaring—but the street ahead of them was empty.

Delancey slammed his fists on the dashboard and screamed his rage out in one terrifying, throat-rending roar.

12

———

ALL THAT IS LIVING SPEAKS TO ME

VISITING hours were over and the patients went back to their beds.

The nurses tried to convince Francis his daughter was safe. He refused go. He was afraid to leave her now that they'd found her after those feverish days. But the staff threatened him with calling security and he had to leave.

IT WENT quiet on the neurology floor. Andrea's room was only illuminated with a small, celadon lamp over the bed.

The first thing she heard was the low, slow beat and hum of her own heartbeat and blood flow. The first thing she felt was her chest expanding and contracting in breaths and the touch of her hospital gown scratching her skin—the weight of the bed cover pushing down on her.

And Andrea heard in her dream: "It's time, Eden."

She opened her eyes and in that same moment the light above her head went off.

Andrea lifted her hands and felt her face. Then, she reached to her wrist and pulled out the cannula. The hole in her arm bled a while and then it closed. She reached between her legs and tore out the urine catheter.

She sat on the bed, trying to understand where she was. She heard millions of sounds, from the corridor, from the other rooms, patients snoring or moaning in their sleep, or TV shows with the apish cries of the anchors and idiotic laughter and ovations, and from the outside: quieter, the hum of night traffic, voices of passersby, the barking of a dog who was happy with his walk as his master had finally gotten back from work. She heard everything. And she felt a strange power and rage within her. It was a really good feeling.

There was something she didn't like here, however. Like buzzing, zapping in her brain. Somehow, she knew what it was: electric current, sizzling in the wires that ran through the walls. It made her anxious. She hated it.

Then she felt a clear, song-like calling in her mind. She knew she had to go and she knew where.

Andrea got out of her bed and walked out of her room into the corridor. The bright, bluish light of neon lamps disappeared as they went off one by one. The hum of electricity declined a bit. Was it her who caused that blackout?

"Hello?" she said.

"Hey! The lights when out!" a nurse said to another in their staff room. Andrea heard her anxious voice. "Check the heart monitors!"

The creak of doors, quick footsteps, cries of alarm.

Andrea put her hand against the cool wall and felt the passage nearby.

The door had an electromagnetic lock; she felt and saw its red, pulsating aura. As soon as she approached it, the aura disappeared and the electromagnet died.

"What is going on?" she wondered. It seemed a part of her knew what she should do while the other part observed in wonder.

"Hey! Is there anyone there? I can't see!" another nurse called in her direction, and she suddenly decided she had to get away from here.

She pulled the door open and stepped into the back staircase.

It was completely dark in there, but with the sharpening of her sight, hearing, touch and intuition, she discovered she could walk well enough.

She heard a small voice from the corner of the staircase.

"One-two, one-two, spin the yarn, spin the yarn, my corner trap, my trap-home, sweet trap-home," somebody whispered.

She stopped and squinted her eyes to see better.

There was a spider in a web, moving its legs quickly and building its web. It froze when it saw her.

"Spider?" she said. She couldn't believe she heard its voice.

"Who are you?" the small voice croaked. "Are you Eden?"

"You can hear me?!"

"Are you Eden?" the spider replied with amazement in its voice.

"I ... yes. I am Eden," she said.

"Savior and protector!" the spider yelled. "I will follow you to the ends of the Earth."

She laughed.

"I don't need you to follow me," she said. "This is amazing."

She felt the calling again, stronger this time. She knew she had to go to the place she saw in her dream, and fast.

"Stay, Eden! Give me your blessing!" the spider called, but she ran downstairs five floors, her muscular legs stronger and springier than ever. She rushed out of the staircase into the hospital lobby, full of bright light and the voices of wounded people waiting to be admitted and the hum of the TV set hanging from the ceiling for them to have something to gape at.

As soon as she set her bare foot in the lobby, the lights and the TV went off, and the people and doctors stood up and began talking, a loud mishmash of frightened voices that hurt her sharpened senses. She cried with pain and covered her ears. Pushing people out of her way, she ran out of the hospital.

She was outside, on the wide stairs, and it was so much better. She inhaled the night air voraciously, but she could taste the pollution on her tongue. Car exhaust pipes. Chimneys. So many lights around.

She went down the steps into the hospital courtyard, a wide alley surrounded with a lawn and some trees. She saw somebody under one of the trees.

It was an androgynous creature. She couldn't say a man or woman; the person was naked, its skin of greenish hue. Twigs and leaves grew out of their body and head.

"Eden!" they said religiously, looking at her with a wide smile. "You came!"

"Who are you?" Andrea asked with hesitation.

"I'm the spirit of this chestnut tree. See my round, spiky chestnuts? I live under the sky, pulling minerals from the soil with my long and thick roots. I drink the power of the sun and rain. The trees of the city waited for you. You will extinguish the Rising Star and restore darkness to the night. We are your servants, indebted to you forever."

Andrea smiled at the spirit too. She knew she should be bewildered, but she no longer reacted like the old her. She was elated at her new powers and possibilities. It felt good to be alive. Life was a force swimming through everything in the world, pulsating, exciting, ecstatic.

But there was no time: she had to go to the place of her watch.

She left the hospital grounds and walked down Minstral Avenue in the direction that called her.

As she walked, the streetlights darkened above her and switched back again after she passed. Her way was surrounded with darkness.

She heard swift, quiet steps, and turned back. She saw three mangy dogs following her. As they got close, they stopped and looked at her.

"Doggies," she said. "What do you want?"

They were ugly and flea-ridden, but strong and bore many scars. The largest of them, who looked like a cross between a golden retriever and boxer, with its snout bearing a huge old scar, stepped ahead.

"We are yours, Eden," he said.

"I have to go for my watch," she said.

"We will protect you," the dog said. "All that is living will."

"Good." She smiled, turned back to the direction she had to go, and went on. And as she walked through the district, more and more dogs joined her. Soon there were a dozen of them, big and small, some of them stray mongrels, some of a good breed who'd escaped through the holes in their homes' fences to follow Andrea.

Suddenly she felt an evil force, something new and disturbing. It came from ahead and was getting closer. She stopped.

AFTER GABRIEL PARKED his mother's car, it took no more than ten steps for him to see Andrea. She was standing in a hospital gown under a dead streetlight. Behind her, he saw a pack of dangerous looking dogs, their eyes gleaming in the dark. Above, he saw bats circling.

"Gabriel! Be careful," he heard Maurice's alarmed voice.

But he was too fascinated to listen. He approached her.

"Andrea?" he said. He thought she looked more beautiful than ever, her hair heavy and curled, falling on her white gown, her skin healthy and smooth, her eyes huge and deep and shining.

"Gabriel," she said and smiled. "It's you. Do you know I like you? You must know."

"You do?" he asked.

"Of course. You didn't notice?"

"Andrea, but, where are you going ... like that?"

Her smile vanished; she shook her head.

"I have to go and keep my watch. You wouldn't believe what's going on."

"Yes...?" Gabriel asked with a bit of fear. Now he thought she looked too intense, not herself, haunted. "What is going on, Andrea?"

"Everything is alive," she said.

"It is?"

"Can't you see? Everything is breathing and growing."

"Okay," he said.

"I can see spirits of nature," she said. "The trees, the animals. They're listening to me, Gabriel? Would you believe it?"

He couldn't believe. But he had to. He could see the dogs and the bats, and now he was closer he saw a circle of moths spinning above her head, like a halo.

"Maurice?" he whispered, but the demon was nowhere to be seen.

"What?" Andrea didn't understand what he said.

"Andrea ... I can see spirits too. And they're listening to me." It came as such a relief. He had found someone like him. And it was the girl he was in love with.

What a blessed night.

"Yes?" she laughed.

"Yes. I can see demons of all things, like cars, clothes, all machines. And they listen to what I tell them. They call me an Ombudsman."

"You are an Ombudsman?" she asked with a new tone in her voice. She looked at him as if she were suddenly afraid.

"Yes..."

Wild anger contorted her face.

"*Ahanari!*" she shouted. "Kill him!"

With an ear-piercing shriek, the bats dived at him, and with a deafening barking the pack of dogs rushed at him. He turned to run, but the first one jumped on his back and he fell to his hands and knees.

He screamed as the dog on his back bit him in the neck. Fortunately, the thick material of his hood protected him some. The other dog bit his hands, another his legs. The bats sat on him looking for pieces of uncovered skin to bite into. He was covered with furious animals, slick with their saliva and his blood.

He screamed for help again.

"Pierre!" he cried. "Pierre!"

His mother's car dashed down the street and smashed into the pack of dogs. Among their yelps and whines, he stopped inches from him, honking at the dogs and flashing the headlights.

Gabriel dropped to the sidewalk. He managed to turn on his back, protecting himself from the biting dogs with one arm and reaching to his hoodie pocket to grab his gun.

He began shooting at them, and some of them jumped away. The cloud of bats and moths lifted off him. Limping, with two dogs hanging from his arms, he pushed through the open door of the car and shut it twice on the two dogs. They yelped and let go.

He closed himself in the car. For a moment, he saw Andrea standing there, looking at him with her haunted wide eyes, before the dogs jumped on the hood of the car and rammed their maws against the windshield.

"Drive away! Drive!" he yelled.

"On it, kid!" Pierre cried. And backed off, made a U-Turn, and crashed through several dogs with screeching tires.

Gabriel fell back on the seat and cried with shock.

"God! God!" he cried. "What was that? Oh God!"

He looked at his hands. They were dark red, glistening with blood.

"Damn!" he cried, as tears of pain rolled down his face. "What was that?"

"Where are we going, son? There's a hospital nearby!" Pierre said.

"No. There's a first-aid kit at the apartment," Gabriel said. "Go there."

"You can get rabies," Pierre said.

"What?"

"Those dogs could have rabies. They didn't look like well-groomed and vaccinated poodles."

"I can't go to a hospital! They'll tell the police," Gabriel said. "Maurice! Will you show up at last?"

"I'm here," a calm voice replied, and the demon appeared in the passenger seat next to him. "Excuse me, Gabriel. I needed to think about what happened."

"Well, what's there to think about? She's like an Ombudsman, but commanding the spirits of nature. Which you didn't even tell me existed!"

"I'm telling you everything I know, okay?"

"Well, I sometimes have doubts about it."

"Ombudsman!" Maurice looked him straight in the eyes. "You don't trust me? After all we've been through?"

Gabriel sighed and wiped his forehead of the blood dripping into his eyes.

"Okay. Okay, Maurice. What should I do now?"

"That's exactly what I'm thinking about."

"Because suddenly I have, like, more problems than ever? Two murderous Princes who are after me and my brother, plus a school friend who wants to kill me with mad dogs, and bats, and whatever else there was eating me..."

"Plus a potential of rabies," Pierre added.

"Thank you, Pierre. Almost forgot about that."

"To answer your question, one thing I would do," said Maurice, "would be to make sure I never meet your school friend again."

"Wouldn't want to come across her in a forest, no sir," Pierre said. "Imagine what she could do to you with wolves and foxes and bears and wild boars."

"Does what happened there change the picture?" Gabriel kept speaking fervently. "That my school friend is now this, I don't know, crazed druid beast master or something? Let's do some thinking. No, I don't think so. Things are unchanged. I still need to protect Matt from the Princes."

"Yes, but Pierre's right," Maurice said calmly. "You need to see a doctor. The rabies vaccination, stitches where you need them. You won't be protecting Matt with foam at your mouth and hydrophobia."

Gabriel looked out the window for a while. They were crossing the Marienstett Bridge over the river, and the houses on the opposite bank and Poselet Island reflected their lit windows in the dark floating water.

"Okay," he said. "What kind of a doctor wouldn't call the police? Do you want me to find a mafia doctor or something?"

"Why don't you call police yourself?" Maurice replied. "Like Senior Agent Delancey. He would know how to arrange it."

"Okay. Li, call him."

"Holy shit, what time is it?" he heard Delancey mutter from the speaker.

"I need some help…"

"Are you alright?" the agent's voice jumped to attention. "Where are you?"

"I'm okay, don't worry, no. I just … I have a bad cut, a dog attacked me, a stray dog. And I need to get some injections, right? And stitches. But I don't want them to call the police, as I'm still a wanted person, right?"

"Okay. Remember the hospital on Vadomski Street, where I stayed? They have a twenty-four-seven E.R. We use it. In the meantime, I'll call them and have everything arranged. Tell the receptionists Agent Delancey sent you. They'll know by then."

13

———

FAREWELL TO THE CHILD

DELANCEY WAITED in the reception area of the hospital, sitting on a plastic chair and dozing off. He woke up as Gabriel came into the room from the surgery and sat next to him.

"Are you alright?" Delancey asked him.

Gabriel nodded.

"I have, like, a hundred stitches." He looked at his bandaged arm and hand. "Now I'm waiting for the injections. Thank you for coming."

"What happened there, son?"

Gabriel went quiet. He thought for a while.

"It seems ... it seems it's not only the things made by us that have their spirits. It seems nature has its spirits as well. And Andrea can command them. She escaped the hospital."

Delancey groaned and covered his eyes.

"Why is it me?" he asked. "I don't even believe in yeti. Do I need to be in the middle of this metaphysical shitstorm?"

"She can command animals. Dogs, bats, birds," Gabriel continued. "They protect her ... and apparently they will kill for her too."

"Why did she want to kill you? You pick on her at school or something?"

"No, I..." Gabriel shook his head. It was difficult. "Agent Delancey, on the contrary."

"Broken heart, maybe?"

"I don't know. I was so delighted she can see the invisible, too, that I shared I command demons ... and she just went mad. Sent those dogs on me."

"Where is she now? Do you know?"

"She was going somewhere. We met by the hospital."

"Well, I don't know what we can do about her, with the Princes on their killing spree. But she's obviously dangerous."

"I don't know if she's dangerous to the others," Gabriel said. "She became aggressive only after I said I was an Ombudsman."

"Okay, but looking at your stitches, I don't think it was a balanced reaction, no?"

"No, you're right."

"So I put her on our lists again, but this time not as missing, as wanted."

Gabriel nodded.

"Don't try to visit her anymore, eh, son?"

"You bet I won't," Gabriel said.

Delancey nodded at patted Gabriel on his leg. "Okay. Wait here for your rabies shot. I will go and thank the doctor who patched you up and tell him to make do without the paperwork."

"Thank you, Agent. "

"As for you, make sure you go and take a proper rest. Stay at home for a few days. I mean, you do have a place to stay...?"

"I do."

Delancey looked at him dubiously. This teenager was something else.

"Agent Delancey?"

"Yes?"

"What about my father? Do you know anything?"

"Not yet, sorry. I made a regular search, but it turned out

nothing. Like he never existed. I asked Oscar to dig a little deeper, but we really had a lot of work recently."

"It's important for me."

"I know. Sorry. I'll remind him tomorrow."

"And the Princes? Are you getting closer to them?"

"I think we almost have them. Don't worry."

Gabriel understood it was a lie.

FRANCIS SLEPT with his phone on the pillow next to his head in case there was some news from the hospital. But it wasn't his phone that woke him up.

He turned onto his back, raised his head and squinted, trying to see in his dark bedroom. He saw a silhouette standing by the open door to the terrace, the door he distinctly remembered closing before going to sleep. He stared at the shadow with his heart beating fast and strong. A burglar. But why did the motion sensors in the back yard not work? Why was Pele quietly lying on his feet, paying no attention to the intruder?

Francis decided in a split second. He sat up and reached quickly to the lamp. It didn't come on. But looking at the strange person, he started to discern long hair and the familiar body shape.

"Andrea?" he asked. "Is that you?"

He got off the bed, moved to the light switch without turning his back to the intruder, and tried the switch several times—to no effect. There was no power.

"Is that you?"

"Yes, Dad," finally came the answer in a creamy voice.

He felt a wave of relief come over him, and then realized the situation was still very wrong.

"What ... what are you doing here? Why aren't you at the hospital?"

"Because I wanted to say goodbye," she said.

He approached her warily. Something was off about her.

She had her old blanket wrapped around her arms. She was still wearing the hospital gown, and he saw her feet were bare.

"I took my blanket," she explained. "Where I'm going, I will need it, I think."

"You came here on your own? You escaped the hospital?"

"I wanted to say goodbye and take the blanket," Andrea said with the same infinite, dreamy calm in her voice. "You can go back to sleep, Dad."

"Andrea ... you are sick, baby. Where do you want to go?"

"I have to go to the Birdflipper, Dad."

"Who is that? Who is the Birdflipper, Andrea? Tell me!"

He grabbed her shoulders.

"Goodbye, Dad."

She turned to go through the open terrace door, but he didn't let her.

"Hey!" he said and pulled her back.

With a sudden growl, and a fit of barking, Pele, their lazy pacifist basset hound, jumped at him from the bed and bit his leg. Francis cried in pain and let Andrea go. In a split second, she was outside, running across their back yard on her long, well-trained legs.

He managed to kick Pele away and ran after her, crying her name. The outside lamps were dark and dead, but he saw her run at great speed towards the wall, climb over it, and disappear on the other side.

He stopped. He knew he had no chance of doing the same. In his mind, he quickly went through the possible routes she could take after scaling the wall. The car!

He ran around the house to the driveway, and only when he saw his car did he remember the keys. Cursing, he ran back to the house through the terrace, grabbed the keys from the tray in the entryway and ran out through the front door.

He jumped into his car and pulled out of their driveway.

He turned left into the darkened road and hit the brakes. There was a whole crowd of house pets, maybe a dozen, blocking the road. He recognized their neighbors' dogs, big and small, their cats, standing in the middle of the road and barring his exit. Their eyes reflected the glow of his headlights.

The road ahead of him, behind the animals, drowned in darkness, and he saw the streetlights going off one by one as Andrea ran by them, getting farther and farther away.

He slammed the horn several times and started to roll slowly towards the animals. The dogs barked, the cats bared their fangs and hissed at him, but they didn't budge. Even when he got so close he began pushing some of them, they didn't flinch. Some dogs bit his front tires.

He shifted the car into reverse and backed off. Then he pressed the pedal to the metal; his engine roared as he evaded the animals in a wide arc through his neighbors' lawn.

Back on the road, the animals chasing him, he could see Andrea ahead, getting closer and closer. She looked back and saw him. She said something.

Two flocks of birds flew off the treetops on both sides of the road, and with loud caws covered the windshield with a living, feathery carpet. He couldn't see a thing. Afraid he would hit her, he slowed down, slammed the windshield with his fist, and then turned on the wipers. The wipers hit the mass of birds but they didn't budge. Some of the birds stepped over them, some just allowed themselves to be pushed aside, while new ones took their place.

He heard her single, distant scream—some word he didn't understand—and his car slowed down to a stop, the engine died, his dashboard grew totally black, as if all power was cut off. He tried to start it several times, pressing the clutch and punching the START button, but nothing happened.

He opened the door and got out of the car.

"Andrea!" he cried in desperation. But the road ahead was empty.

With a flutter, the mass of crows covering his car dissolved as they flew up into the dark sky, screaming. Behind him, his neighbors walked out of their suburban homes, woken in the middle of the night by the sound of house alarms, animals noises, and Francis' car engine.

ANDREA RAN like she was carried by the wind, her legs doing the task on their own, one-two, one-two, her hair flowing in the air behind her. She passed by houses, fields, and crossroads, and finally she felt tired as she ran up onto a hill outside town. The hill rose above a wide field. She could see little houses of a nearby village. She dropped to her knees under a weeping willow, and its spirit, a young woman with green hair hanging to the ground, leaned over her and asked softly, "Eden? Are you ill?"

She shook her head.

"I'm afraid," she whispered into the grass. "I don't know what's going to happen to me."

The Willow smiled gently.

"I've been standing on this hill for a hundred years and more, Eden, and I know. What happens, it happens. And what happens, it passes. Hills, roads, people. There's no need to fear."

Andrea nodded, sat up and wiped her face. She saw a flicker of yellow eyes as a fat, round cat walked out the from behind the tree.

"What are you doing here, Eden?" the cat asked her in a low, female voice.

"I'm on my way to what I have to do. I had to leave every-thing behind and it was ... very hard," Andrea answered. A single yellow light appeared in one of the windows in the village. Somebody had to get up very early.

"You're like a dog, eh?" asked the cat with a smile. "Home, home, home. Master, oh master. I'm different. My home is where I hide at night. I don't know what I will eat tomorrow or where I'll be at. But tonight it's different."

"Why?"

"Look at me. Can't you see? I have little babies in my womb. I lay with a wild black cat one wild night. Now I'm going to have babies. I'm going to this village you see to find a home. I will meow and act nice and lean against their legs so they have mercy and lend me a warm corner in a barn or a cellar. I need a home and I need humans to bring me food for my little ones so they survive. Are you expecting, Eden?"

"What?" Andrea smiled. "No."

"Then why do you need a home? Are you a dog?"

"I'm not."

"So go follow your destiny. Go to the place you've been called to."

Andrea nodded. She reached out her hand and petted the cat's head. It shivered with pleasure and purred.

"Good luck in finding a home," Andrea said.

"Good luck in fulfilling your destiny, Eden," the cat answered.

The Willow smiled.

Andrea got up to her feet and walked on, to the north, carrying her old blanket to keep her warm during the coming nights of unknown.

14

THE CRUELEST ANIMAL

DELANCEY WALKED over to Ali's coffee stand in Demianov Square, where NBI headquarters was located. Ali's coffee was the one bright point of his every working day. He had long ago decided in secret that when Ali disappeared from the square, he'd retire.

"What's new, Agent?" asked Ali, turning on the espresso machine among the clouds of steam and loud hissing.

"People ain't no good," answered Delancey. "But I guess that's not really new, eh?"

"You came from a different direction than usual."

"Yeah, I'm sleeping at the office these days."

"There's a funny gentleman fifteen feet behind you, covering his face with a newspaper. Please don't turn," Ali said casually, setting up the paper cup. "He's been here for fifteen minutes. Not many people stand in the middle of the square pretending to read a paper. I think he's coming here now."

"Andrew Delancey?" said a theatrical, lisping voice behind him.

Delancey swiftly put his hand on the butt of his gun under his jacket and turned to face the stranger.

It was a tall man in a long, gray, plastic raincoat. His face was covered with one of those toy red noses with glasses and twirly mustache. On his head he had what quite obviously was a wig of curly black hair.

"Who's asking?" said Delancey coolly. "You're with CAISA, eh? What's with the masquerade, bud?"

"What masquerade? I just wanted to say hello!" cried the stranger goofily, spreading out his arms—Delancey immediately noticed his hands were empty—and embraced the agent, patting him on his back.

"Move away!" Delancey shouted, stepping back and getting on one knee and at the same time ripping his gun out of the holster and aiming at the man. "Don't move!"

"Uh-oh..." The man stepped from one foot to the other. "Uh-oh ... I think I'm not welcome here!"

He turned and dashed into the crowd of commuters filling Demianov Square.

"Get on the ground! On the ground, everyone!" yelled Delancey, trying to aim his gun at the raincoat flashing between passersby, but it was hopeless: the few people who could even hear and understand him just stopped and looked at him like idiots. He cursed, lowered his gun, and pushed through the crowd, chasing the strange man. He got to another block and couldn't see him. He kept looking around, his heart beating fast, scanning the faces moving by.

Suddenly something black flew at him and covered his head, and he heard laughter; he fought with the black material and ripped it away, realizing it was the man's raincoat.

He looked in the windows of surrounding office buildings above, at the street busy with cars, and the stream of people passing him from all directions. Maybe if he had a helicopter, right here, right now, he'd be able to get the stranger...

He cursed again, picked up the cheap plastic raincoat from the sidewalk, and turned to go back to NBI headquarters. He saw two huge blokes in black suits, flushed from following him, disoriented, and keeping their hands on the guns under their jackets. CAISA.

"Thanks for your nothing, morons," he snapped. "One time we could use your help…"

He passed by them and went back to the NBI building.

"Stanley, I need you and your guys to go over the feed from the square," he said to the old janitor in the lobby and showed him the raincoat. "We're looking for a tall man wearing this coat, in a black wig. Give me a call when you have something."

"Hi, Chief," Beatrice greeted him from her desk as he passed the bullpen. "You look as if you saw a ghost."

He didn't answer, and she didn't press on, because her phone rang.

The guy could have been a madman. But for some reason the encounter shook Delancey. He felt that something really bad had happened.

He had only just managed to sit down at his desk when Beatrice appeared in his door. He looked up at her with a question in his eyes.

"It's one of the families," she said quietly.

THEY STOPPED NEXT to Pete's car. Delancey looked at the one-family house, one of the locations the bureau had reserved for its witness protection program—a sandbox, a tricycle, and the front lawn with his agents and cops standing in silence. He got a strong urge to turn away and never come back. His hand felt weak, unable to open the door to get out of the car. He didn't want to go there.

Confused by his reluctance, Pete knocked on the window.

"Andrew?" Beatrice said.

Delancey nodded and got out of the car. So did Beatrice.

"First, there's the security. They were guarded by Ruslan's

anti-terrorists. Over there, in the black car," Pete said. He seemed more grim than usual.

Delancey saw one of the men on the lawn was Ruslan. They nodded to each other.

He walked over to the black car. The two SWAT operators sat in the front seat, with their heads bent back and both the barrels of their guns deep in their mouths. They were missing the backs of their heads.

"How did that happen?" Delancey said. "Any theories?"

"Somebody forced them to shoot their brains out," Pete shrugged. "That's all I can say for now."

"That's all I can see, too," snapped Delancey.

Pete let that go and looked at his feet.

"Then there's the family."

Delancey nodded.

"Go on"

"There's a sauna in the basement. They appear to have been locked in there. The sauna door didn't want to give in. We had to break it down, and, well, they had been locked in there, and somebody set the temperature really high. We had to cut off the main power to cool it down. Didn't even know saunas could get that hot."

They kept silent. Delancey turned to Beatrice.

"You can stay here."

She nodded, biting her lip.

"Thank you, Chief."

Delancey went into the house. It was furnished simply and comfortably, with the protected, troubled people who might temporarily live there in mind. He passed a grim cop at the stairs to the basement.

The heat was unbearable.

He went downstairs. The sauna was in the corner of the large game room, a stall of wooden walls, and the remains of a door hanging on the hinges. The smell was stronger here, and he recognized it at last: boiled meat. He stood in the game room, alone in the hot basement, with sweat dripping down his shirt collar, and he looked at the door he had to go through to see the crime scene.

He couldn't do it. He had seen so many atrocities already. But this time his whole body was saying no. Something had snapped.

 on as Delancey walked out of the house. His face looked like all the light had gone. He turned to Pete.

"Swipe down the house for evidence. Question the neighbors. Establish what happened with Ruslan's men."

The agent nodded. Then Delancey turned to Beatrice. His voice was soft and void of emotion.

"There's only one message we need to get across to high command. We can't protect anyone. Advise all the families of children kidnapped by Bolani to be moved out of town. But if the fuckers found one of our safe houses, I don't know if that would be any helpful. Let all personnel involved in the Boleani investigation know that they can take days off, can lock themselves in a bunker, whatever, I don't know. Tell the boss ... we can't protect anyone."

"And you?" Beatrice asked.

"I'm going home for tonight. I have to take a rest. I'm..." He shrugged. "I need to rest."

He stared her in the eyes and she realized how true that was.

"Okay."

"And I need to prepare ... for whatever more is coming."

15

TAKEN

D ELANCEY GOT on a bus and went to Ursenev, the bedroom district of Los Maines, to his small one-man studio in a sky-high apartment tower.

He got brain zaps on the way. Small, irritating snaps of energy he kept getting since going off Atroposine. A herald of a really bad attack of withdrawal symptoms.

It was dark when he got off the bus. He bought some Jack Daniels at the local drugstore and went home.

In his head, he kept seeing the severed leg baking in the oven. As soon as he chased it out of his mind, he thought about the family locked in the searing hot sauna. Somehow the fact he didn't see them made it even worse. That was a mistake.

He sat in the living room, on the sofa, drinking and watching TV, the stream of chaotic images from a loud, hedonistic civilization he was no part of. Laughing families competing for money prizes, crawling and jumping over obstacles. First kisses of lovers on a dating reality show. Wild Ibiza parties. He felt like an alien watching a transmission from another planet.

He felt alright chasing the Stellen Street Kidnapper, like a hound tracking a deer. Now he just felt hopeless and helpless. Each strange new thing happening around him was a blow. The world was chaotic, a playground of forces beyond anyone's control, and he was so tired. If the world made no sense, what impact did his prohibition make? Wasn't it better to just try and feel good for as long as possible, helping others in the meantime, even if it meant an addiction? Was life without addiction any good? If it wasn't, then why torment himself?

He reached for his phone, found the contact. His phone kept acting strange; it lagged. Delancey looked at the contact's number, sighed, and threw the phone across the room.

He went to the bathroom to put his head under cold water. He screamed, looking in the mirror and squishing his temples between his fists. He couldn't bear it any longer.

His fingers were wet with sweat and slipping on the screen of his phone when he found it and selected the long-ignored contact. It took a while for the lagging phone to call the number.

"Well I never," said the unpleasant, nasal voice in the phone. "My best client is back."

"Hi, Leonardo," Delancey said. "I was wondering, maybe I could use a bit of A."

"Oh."

There was a moment of silence that felt like ages for Delancey, who had been shivering with desire from the moment he decided to give in to temptation. He licked his lips.

"Leonardo? Are you there?"

"I am ... but I would like you to know, things have changed."

"Changed? How?"

"Well, it seems the stream ran dry some time ago. Harder and harder to get your hands on A."

"How much do you want?"

"I'm not saying that to haggle, mate. That the truth. The usual channels stopped delivering."

"Come on. How is that possible? No demand?"

"It's a different kind of substance, dude, okay? I used to get it from folks that don't deal in the normal stuff. I don't like them very much, an ugly bunch. Apparently, something happened that made them lose a large portion of production. Maybe a police bust or something."

"Alright, Leonardo, I know what you're doing. You just want me to beg, don't you? Is that what you're doing?"

"No, man! Who needs your begging, fuck's sake? I just don't have the stuff."

"Come on. Leo. I can make it worth your while. Don't tell me you can't find it."

There was another moment of silence.

"Maybe, just maybe, I could scrape something for you ... but it's going to cost extra. I need to reach out to somebody, and it's the middle of the night, for Christ's sake."

"Leonardo, I would be very grateful. You can do it. You're the man, aren't you, Leonardo?"

"Two-fifty for one serving. I can get you five."

"You get it."

"See you at the overpass in thirty minutes."

Leonardo disconnected. Delancey's heart beat fast like a lover unbuttoning his girlfriend's blouse for the first time. He opened the drawer of his dresser so fast he broke its fixing. Dug in a pile of socks and took out an envelope. He had around a thousand in crumpled notes. Leonardo would give him a discount for sure. If not, he'd just take four. Or five. But would leave him his watch as a collateral.

"I'm doing the right thing," he muttered to himself. 'It will make me a better investigator. Clarity of thought, energy in action. I will be able to help the people better. I can't be so self-ish, fretting about my damn health all the time as if it were all that mattered."

He tore his trousers in the crotch he pulled them up so fast. "Fucking things," he muttered. He threw on a black windbreaker and left his apartment. He couldn't wait for the elevator to arrive, and so took the stairs.

The overpass Leonardo mentioned was the usual place where Delancey picked his orders up from the dealer. It was half an hour on foot, so Delancey was happy to see a night bus standing right at the bus stop next to his building, all lit up and inviting, its three pairs of doors wide open.

"Wait!" he cried and broke into a run.

As he jumped into the bus, it huffed; the engine roared and the doors closed with a hiss. Delancey dropped onto a seat with a sigh of contentment. The bus pulled into traffic.

It was three stops away. Delancey looked around the inside of the bus with a nervous smile, impatient to meet Leonardo.

Just then, he noticed something strange. There were no other passengers. No night partygoers, no old, retired folks coming back from mysterious retirement meetings, no punks, no hobos. Nobody. And it was driving too fast.

Delancey looked towards the driver's area, but the driver's seat was in a separate compartment, divided from the rest of the bus by a plastic wall.

Outside, they drove past a bus stop without so much as touching the brakes.

"Hey!" he cried in the direction of the driver. "Mind slowing down a bit?"

There was an ugly grinding sound as they hit a car in the left lane. Honking, the bus went faster and faster.

"Are you crazy in there?" Delancey yelled. He got up and tried to reach the driver. grabbing the seat backs, step by step, staggering towards the front of the bus.

Just then, the bus took a sudden turn and Delancey hit the window. He felt a prick of bad pain in his back and fell down. Grabbing onto a rail, he got to his feet, reached for his pistol, and took a look into the driver's compartment.

"Hey, you—" he cried, and the words froze in his mouth as he saw there was no driver inside.

The night bus was driving on its own, hurtling towards an

unknown destination, veering to the left and right, taking rapid turns and bumping other cars.

Delancey yanked on the plastic door to the driver's seat. It was locked. He hung from his hands from a bar overhead and kicked the lock with both feet. It broke. He barged through the door, grabbed the wheel and pressed on the brake pedal with all his might. The pedal went all the way down to the floor and the bus didn't react. Delancey moved the wheel and it had absolutely no impact on the vehicle.

He was being kidnapped by an unmanned night bus.

He reached for his phone, chose Beatrice's number, and put it to his ear.

A terrible digital shriek exploded in his ear, sending a needle of pain deep inside and hurting his brain. Delancey cried out and checked the screen. App icons swam across the screen amid crackles of some interference. Useless. He remembered his phone had been acting strange since this morning.

The bus got onto a freeway and reached its maximum speed. The houses ended and darkness engulfed them, nothing to see other than streetlamps flashing past on both sides, and the cracked asphalt of the road ahead illuminated by the bus's headlights.

They were outside the city limits, speeding through the deserted wasteland that spread for miles from Los Maines' southern border.

One by one, Delancey tried the buttons controlling the doors. It was safe to say none of the bus controls worked.

He scrambled out of the driver's seat back to the passengers area. He reached the front door, and with much difficulty, being thrown to and fro by the bus's skidding, he managed to open a small compartment over the door for the red safety lever. He grabbed it and pulled as strong as it could. But the door didn't open.

"Okay, so this is the game we're playing," he whispered,

looking around the bus again. He saw what he searched for above one window: a red glass-breaking hammer in an emergency case.

He got to it, ripped out the little hammer, and smashed the nearest window. With a great noise, the window broke into a spiderweb of cracks. He hit again and a huge portion of it fell out onto the road. A strong, cold wind fell inside, carrying in clouds of desert dust, making him squint.

He pushed his head through the hole and looked outside, his hair flying all around his head on the wind. Flashing in his field of vision, the roadside was full of sharp rocks. He would scrape his skin to bloody meat if he tried to jump out here at the speed they were going.

Just then, the force of momentum threw him against the opposite wall as the bus took a sharp turn to the left, onto a dirt road. The vehicle trembled so much Delancey thought he would lose all his teeth, or break his neck his head shook so bad.

There were no more streetlights; they drove through darkness, but the bus had to go slower here than on the highway, and Delancey saw his chance in that.

He ran at the smashed window full-speed and, protecting his head with his arms, took a leap through the hole, into the dark.

He rolled mid-air and hit the ground as he intended—with his left shoulder. In case he got incapacitated, he preferred to have his right hand operational. The ground was hard but there were no rocks, so apart from some bruises and bad scratches he appeared to be fine.

He stood up as fast as he could and began running in the opposite direction, to the distant lights of the highway.

He quickly heard the roar of the engine behind him. The ground ahead became illuminated with pale blue headlights.

He turned to see, and sure enough, the bus was racing straight at him. It looked surreal, the city bus, fully lit inside, speeding at him across the dark wasteland.

It was useless to run. He stood there facing the bus, waiting for it to come closer so he could jump aside and evade the hit.

But the bus went straight by him without any intention of hitting him. Delancey hesitated, but soon enough it was apparent what was going on: the bus took a wide U-turn and sped at him, determined to drive him to their destination despite everything.

"Holy shit," Delancey cried. He turned back and began running into the desert. He was limping, panting and soaked in sweat. His lungs burned as he gasped for the cold night air, when he saw their destination not far away.

On the horizon, among slag heaps, bathed in dim moonlight, there rose an ominous shape of a large barn or warehouse, lonely in the middle of the desert.

The bus stopped and Delancey dropped to his knees, exhausted. He was catching his breath desperately.

He sat on the coarse sand and tried his phone again. The screen was black and didn't react to his attempts of turning it on.

Delancey cursed and got to his feet.

He took his gun out and looked at the black building.

"Okay. Let's have it, then," he whispered. Hunched down, he began stealing towards the warehouse. His heart beat crazy fast. He could feel the waves of blood pulsating in his head.

It was quiet around the warehouse. Only the wind rustled among the silver, thick-grained dunes of Los Maines Desert, and whistled through the cracks between the corrugated sheets of the warehouse, playing over the metal lines that ran along its roof and down the walls—lightning rod wires, maybe.

Delancey stood in the shadow of the warehouse, five feet from its huge sliding door.

"Hello?" he called out eventually. His voice was a croak. But he had to do something, couldn't take any more waiting. "What are you playing, eh?"

No answer. He looked back and saw the night bus waiting

among the dark dunes, a lonely island of light, like a ghost of the city he'd left behind.

"Pro-active. That's the way you do it, Andrew," he growled to himself. He grabbed the handle on the corrugated sheet door and gave it a strong pull with an angry cry.

The door slid far open and hit its block with a loud metallic noise. Delancey jumped back in a wide stance, aiming straight ahead into the warehouse with his gun.

It was lit with hissing halogen lamps that hung high on the ceiling ... and the whole large space inside was empty, apart from a metal table in the middle. There was something lying on the table.

Aiming left and right and behind, and at the shadows in the corners, his heartbeat pounding in his temples, Delancey made his way to the table and took a look.

What he saw shook him.

A small syringe with a white label, an object he knew so well. His nervous system spat out an intoxicating wave of endorphins, oxytocin, and dopamine at the sight. He felt like a scared child who finds his mother and she embraces him.

A dose of Atroposine.

"Huh?" he said into the shadows, and coughed, and spat on the ground. "Are you fucking making fun of me? Eh? Come out! Damn come out and show yourselves!"

His gun outstretched before him, he marched all around the warehouse, looking behind every pillar and every corner, ready to kill.

There was nobody.

He stood for a few seconds, wondering.

Then he shrugged and went out of the warehouse.

He started walking back towards the highway, towards the city manifesting itself with a faint shimmering aurora on the horizon.

He passed by the bus, dark now and shut down.

And he doubled in two, and his shoulders shook, as he stopped and started to cry.

He screamed with rage and wiped away his tears. He stared ahead, breathing hard, then closed his eyes, shook his head, whispered: "No..." He hesitated one more moment, then turned back once again and went back to the warehouse.

He could hear his excited breathing, small whistles coming out of his lungs, as he rolled up his sleeve, smacked on his vein and pumped his fist, and finally he sent the Atroposine into his bloodstream and dropped to his knees in the ecstasy of his return to paradise. Andrew Delancey was one with the world again. He saw what had come to pass and what he had to do next with calm clarity.

But then the lights went off.

And he understood that he had fucked up.

VOICES IN THE DARK

THE DOOR SHUT and the warehouse fell into complete darkness. It was no different whether he had his eyes open or closed shut. He could see nothing.

He crouched with his gun outstretched, aiming into the pitch black.

He heard the first giggle. High-pitched, malicious, deriding.

And the second one, coming from a different direction.

"Who are you?" he yelled. "Don't come any closer ... or I shoot!"

"He's going to shoot!" screamed a voice.

"Oh no, I have wetted myself from fear!" answered the other one, choking with laughter. "Mercy!"

"We gonna die!" cried the first voice.

"Oh, woe is us!"

"I say, you're so trigger-happy, Agent. It's shoot this, shoot that with you. You even tried to shoot me dead this morning, when I just wanted to hug you and connect to your ugly little phone. Would you really kill for that? You inhuman prick? Shoot, shoot, shoot!"

By the direction of the voices, Delancey sensed the two men circling him.

He started slowly moving towards where he believed the door should be. He planned to get there unnoticed to try opening it and shooting the strangers as soon as he was able to see them.

"And where are *you* going?" a voice asked.

He aimed at where it came from and he shot. *Bang!* The bullet hit the metal wall with a plume of sparks. In the light from the muzzle flash, he saw a human form to the right of where he shot at, a long-haired, tall man. He shot where he stood and in the next flash he saw there was nobody there.

The third flash came from a powerful blow to the head he received from behind.

He fell, trapping the hand with the gun underneath his chest as someone jumped on him and knelt on his shoulders. Before he managed to push himself up, he felt a prick in his neck and a quick burn of pain under his skin. He'd been injected with something.

The attacker got off him and ran away.

Delancey got to his feet, shooting into the darkness three times, the discharges so loud he couldn't hear anything apart from ringing in his ears ... until he felt an overwhelming weakness, and his legs grew soft and he fell down again.

He couldn't move.

His limbs didn't answer the commands coming from his brain.

After a minute or so, somebody grabbed his arm and turned him over so he was facing up.

"Oooooh, Senior Agent Delancey," a mocking voice said with a lisp. His hearing was coming back. "You're an animal."

"A sexy beast!" exclaimed the second voice. "Makes me want to pull down my pants, jerk off and cum in fountains!"

They laughed.

"Pervert," said the first voice. "Mister Perverto. That's you."

"I take offense to that and I fart with offended dignity."

They laughed again. Delancey squinted, hoping to see at least a shadow of the men. Then he felt a blow to his head from the side; somebody had kicked him.

"Ugly man! Ugly man!" cried the Lisp. "Shooting at us! Bad."

"Badso Badderson."

"Makes me want to, I don't know, cut you or something, Agent Delancey."

"You killed the Dowleys?" Delancey asked, and felt the second kick to his head, left ear this time; the pain squeezed some tears from his eyes and he heard more ringing.

"Who exactly told you that you can ask us questions? Baffles me, really."

"Yeah. You're the star of this interview. Not us."

Somehow this made them laugh even harder.

"You, you guys have a sense of humor, a knack for jokes," Delancey said into the darkness, and felt a taste of blood in his mouth. They didn't kick him in his teeth, so that worried him that he might have some organ damage. "I like that. And I'm not asking any more questions. Don't want to cause any problems. I think I can answer whatever questions you have, however, and then ... ouch!" He felt someone grab him by the head and another injection in his neck.

"Shut up!" said the Lisp impatiently. "You're not on a stage making a speech or something."

"What did you just give me?" Delancey asked. There was a snake of terror uncoiling in his stomach. His body started to tremble and he could do nothing to stop it. "Let me go! I won't give you any more trouble. I will call off my people..."

A blow of primordial fear caused by the third drug they had injected him with shook his whole body. He cried. He was about to die. He had never been this afraid in his whole life.

"Please..." he begged. "I'm afraid. I'm so afraid."

"That's a natural state for a human," said the second voice coldly. "Why shouldn't you be afraid? You're very weak. Dependent on things your ancestors made, without even being able to control them. Your life is quite short and shitty."

"You're afraid, Agent Delancey," repeated the first voice. "Do you like that?"

"No ... I don't like that ... please..."

"Hm, strange. Because I like it when you're afraid."

"I will give you everything."

"Everything?"

"Yes. Whatever you want. Just make it stop."

"Oh well! I thought you liked injecting substances. Maybe you want some Atroposine instead?"

"Yes! Please!

"Hm. On second thought, maybe not. Maybe later. Maybe whenever you need some Atroposine, you can call us, and help us, and you'll get some. Sounds like an idea?"

"Yes!"

"You're such an agreeable person! I like that much more than how we started, with all that shouting and shooting. Andrew, there is one thing that interests us. You know Ricko Boleani? That simple chap who lived in a ruin minding his own small business until you came and chased him away and had him killed at the airport?"

"Ricko Boleani..." Delancey repeated. He felt relief he could help his tormentors. "Yes, of course."

"Of course. So, it's not like we're sad you killed him or anything. A repulsive fellow! Plump and ugly. He had, however, one small thing we're interested in. A stupid old thing he used to put on his plump ugly head to make children like him."

"A mask!" Delancey said. "He had a mask that made you look like ... the most loved person to the people who saw you."

"Yes! You are indeed helping! Your word is worth its weight in gold!" said the Lisp.

"Words don't weigh anything, dummy," said the other one.

"Senior Agent's words do, and you're a dummy yourself," replied the Lisp. "Senior Agent...?"

Delancey felt a cold hand stroke his cheek. He shut his eyes even though he couldn't see anything anyway.

"We would very much like to have that mask, you know? We'd take it and just be gone from here."

"Yes, it's not like we like it here."

"Precisely. It's just we have no choice. We have to have that mask, Agent Delancey. We've been looking for it without much success. Now, we're coming to the question on which depends whether you get some more of that sweet Atroposine or some more of that bad, fear-inducing Koloton. The mask, Andrew. Can you tell us where it is?"

"I wish I knew. It got lost during the fight at the airport. I don't know. Swear to God."

"*God!*" one of them repeated, and they laughed like mad hyenas.

"Shut up," said the other one after a while of laughter. "Okay. What else can we give you. Hmmmm..."

"Give me A," Delancey whispered.

"He wants A! But you're not helping, so why should I give you what you want?"

"Give him the Happy Snake."

"Oh. That's an idea."

Delancey screamed as he was held by his head again and another needle pierced his neck.

17

BLOOD IN THE WATER

"Agent Delancey calling," said Li gently, standing over the sofa.

Gabriel opened his eyes; it took him a while to understand what was happening.

Right, the old lady's apartment. He spent most of yesterday there, suffering from fever, headache, and pain in his arm from where he got the rabies immunoglobulin shot. He got out from under the blanket and crossed the room to the window, looking out at the orphanage. Seemed calm. A policeman smoked outside the front gate.

"Do you want to answer that?" Li asked.

"Yes, on speaker," Gabriel said. "Hello?"

"Gabriel!" he heard Delancey's happy voice. "Nice to hear you. It's such a good day."

"What's going on, Agent Delancey?"

"I'm happy to say I solved our problems,' Delancey laughed. "Everything will be fine. You'll be safe, and Matt, and we'll have no more problems in Los Maines."

"What do you mean?"

"As I said, no more problems. I had it settled. There's just one thing we need."

"And that is...?"

"The mask. I know you took it from Boleani Junior. Let's meet, okay? Just take the mask with you."

"I'm not sure I understand. Even if I had it ... how is it going to help us?"

"I can't explain over the phone. Please, trust me. We saved each other's skin more than one time, right?"

Gabriel was silent for a moment.

"That's right, Agent, but ... it's a strange call."

"Because it's a strange solution. But it will work. Kid, listen ... do you want Matt to be safe and nobody ever bothering you two again? See me in the Old Port, at Old Jose's. We'll grab some breakfast and close the whole deal."

The call ended. Maurice appeared and gave Gabriel a very dubious look.

"I wouldn't go there. As you said yourself, it was a weird conversation."

Gabriel thought for a while. "Agent Delancey saved our lives," he said finally. "What else can I do? Sit here in the stink of mothballs and wait for them to come for me or my brother?"

An hour later, Gabriel walked along the cracked, dark waterfront promenade of the Old Port. It was a sunny but windy day, and the ocean smashed its waves against the bulwark with a roar and hiss of foam. Gabriel saw Old Jose's in the distance, a wooden hut with a neon sign on the roof, surrounded by wooden tables and white plastic chairs. The seagulls cried and circled above the restaurant, ready to dive for some leftovers, but there was only one client.

Agent Delancey sat at one of the tables, looking at Gabriel with a wide smile. His face was bright with no signs of worry. It was the first time Gabriel had seen the agent so cheerful, so he felt a trace of hope. Maybe there really was a way to escape the two Princes, and the mask he had in his hoodie's front pocket really was the key? He had kept it hidden from Delancey, though he didn't really know why. It wasn't like he had any good use for it.

Delancey waved at him.

"Sit down," he said with a smile, and pushed an old, laminated piece of paper towards him. The Old Jose's menu. Delancey already had black coffee in a big, chipped cup. "They have great fish and chips, but maybe it's too early. For breakfast, a shrimp and mayo sandwich looks great, eh? Do you drink coffee or are you too young?"

"I do," Gabriel said. "Agent Delancey, I—"

"Oh! Here comes the waiter." Delancey nodded at a scruffy young man in a striped, white-and-blue t-shirt walking towards them from the restaurant. "You know you can tell how good a restaurant is by how criminal the waiters look? This is no exception. I love this joint."

Gabriel noticed how Delancey's eyes were glassy. The agent had a big yellow-and-black bruise on his cheekbone. He moved and talked with certainty Gabriel had never seen in him before. He laughed and chatted, and somehow he moved either too fast —faster than a normal man—or too slow, freezing at some points. It was a scary sight.

"You're orderin'?" asked the waiter, staring at them without a shadow of a smile.

"Indeed we are, pal!" Delancey said, and took the menu from Gabriel and began studying it. "I'll have ... deviled eggs ... and toast with sardines ... Gabriel?"

"Just coffee," said Gabriel. "With milk."

"You're not eating? You have to try their food!" Delancey said, his eyes shining. He licked his lips.

"I'm not really hungry," Gabriel said. Truth be told, he didn't even want the coffee; he just wanted to stand up and get away from here as soon as possible.

The waiter nodded and went back into the hut.

"Okay. Here's the deal ... but maybe you want to wait for coffee?"

"No, please go ahead, Agent."

"Okay. Listen. I made a deal with them."

"You did what?" Gabriel whispered, his heart pounding against his chest like a sledgehammer.

"Yeah, don't be a child. You can reason with anyone. I was too stupid and too violent. Violence isn't the answer. You can always strike a deal with someone." Delancey licked his lips again. Gabriel noticed a drop of sweat trailing down the agent's forehead.

"And the deal is...?" he asked carefully.

"The mask," whispered the agent. "They want the mask."

"But how do you know? You ... you spoke with them?"

"Last night. They took me for a ride out of town." Delancey laughed and combed his hair back with his hand, and Gabriel noticed dry drops of blood around his ear. "No problem. We talked at this warehouse or something. They lost their temper at the beginning, but then we got all civilized. You know, I don't blame them. Everyone has their reasons. They let me go in the end. My phone worked again. I called a taxi and came here. Listen to what the deal is, though. You give them the mask, they pack their stuff and leave. And we never hear from them again."

Delancey chortled uncontrollably, and it became obvious to Gabriel that he was deep, very deep under the influence of some mind-altering drug. He stared at him in horror.

"You met with the Princes?" Gabriel stood up. "Can't you understand? You sold us. All is lost, Agent Delancey. Everything you have on you ... everything ... is now spying on us!"

"Gabriel!" he heard Maurice's alarming cry coming from his wristband.

He turned to the Old Jose's entrance. They stood there. Two tall men in white suits sprinkled with the blood of the restaurant's staff, their hair long and blond, their skin pale like marble. They smiled innocently, beautiful, like two angels.

"What have you done?" Gabriel whispered to Delancey, who stared at the Princes like an idiot, frowning and trying to understand through the haze of intoxication.

"Hey," Delancey said dumbly. "You're here?"

The Princes approached their table. They could be twins, their faces differing in only very small details, like the length of a nose or a black mole on a cheek. They moved with grace, like ballet dancers, and they kept smiling gently at the drugged agent and terrified teenager.

"Very perceptive of you, Agent," said one of them, and the other chortled. "Indeed we're here."

The second one made a sad face. "I'm afraid you won't get your order any moment soon. The service here seems very sluggish. No movement at all."

Gabriel looked at the dark red spots on their white suits. Fresh blood. His mind raced, searching for ways of dealing with the two murderers.

The Princes sat on the chairs and gave him one of their smiles.

"I don't think we got to know each other yet?" one of them said. "We thought poor old Ricko was the only Ombudsman in this godforsaken country of yours."

"Well, and here's me," Gabriel answered in a calm, quiet voice. "And who are you?"

They looked at each other.

"We're ... Laurel and Hardy."

"Yes. That's our names. I'm Hardy, he's Laurel."

"No, the other way around!"

"Sorry."

The two men broke into laughter.

"You're Princes," Gabriel said, and they stopped.

"Oh. That's intriguing. You know about Princes. So, who are the Princes exactly, young Ombudsman?"

"I'm not at school, and this is not a test," Gabriel replied. "It's enough to know you've killed innocent people, and I'm disgusted Agent Delancey wanted to strike a deal with you."

"Well, wait there," Delancey interrupted, "I have my own mind. It's a good deal. Let's try and reach an agreement, okay? No need for any more violence in this city."

"Be quiet, doggie," a Prince said. "Or you won't get any more bones."

"Why do you need the mask?" Gabriel asked.

"You have some courage, buddy, talking to us like that," a Prince said. "But I like it." He looked at his companion. "Tell them."

"Really?"

"Yeah. Why not? It's a funny story."

The second Prince chortled.

"Okay? Well, friends, there's a very curious chemical substance that makes many people happy. It is extracted from the spine of a living, suffering human. And the substance is never quite as good as when it comes from a human tormented by someone he or she loves the most in the world. That's the use our poor old Ricko discovered for that strange mask he found. And now he's gone, and that perfect blend of that magic stuff is gone with him. But not all is lost, right? The secret sauce. The mask. With that we could make more of that very best Atroposine in the world. We miss it, and many powerful people miss it too."

"What?" Delancey whispered with his thin, pale lips.

"Young Boleani made Atroposine in his basement, extracting it from the kidnapped kids. He wore the mask to appear to them as their parent, or whoever they liked the most, get it?" The other Prince seemed impatient with Delancey's slow comprehension. "That's how he got the best flavor. You should understand. You're a connoisseur of A, aren't you, Agent?"

Delancey's face froze in one expression, half astonishment, half terror. The Princes laughed so hard they had to hold their bellies.

"You should see yourself," one of them managed to say through the bouts of laughter. "What? Don't like A anymore? Come on. It's good stuff."

The lisping Prince turned to the other one and whispered theatrically:

"I think Agent Delancey doesn't find it funny he injected himself with a tormented baby's juice. As a law enforcer, that could sting."

"And you killed for the mask?" Gabriel said. "Mother, father, their son?"

"Well, we were gathering information. We came here, to Los Maines, feeling lost, like children in the mist. We needed to ask some questions. As for the family, we were in a very good mood, and there are sometimes victims when we are in a good mood."

"We're bad."

"Ouch. I'm afraid sometimes we are."

The two Princes looked at each other and smiled with their perfect white teeth. Sunlight sprinkled gold dust in their hair.

"Besides, we need to clean up this whole deal. Those children ... they are dangerous, man."

"Why?" Gabriel asked.

They only smiled in response.

"And you destroyed my apartment," he continued.

"Please, don't take offense to that. It was so old and ugly."

The other Prince shrugged. "I'm getting bored. Give us the mask and we will kill you already, okay?"

Gabriel looked at Delancey. The agent stared at the table with wide open eyes, motionless, paralyzed with new knowledge, or maybe by the many drugs in his system.

"The mask. I'm dying to see it."

The Prince reached his hand out to Gabriel.

"Li ... now," Gabriel said.

"What?" The Prince raised his eyebrows.

"Here's your mask," Gabriel said. He took out his gun from the front pocket of his hoodie, aimed at the Prince's face, and pulled the trigger.

The trigger didn't move an inch. It was as if it was blocked.

A smile appeared on the Prince's face.

"Oh no," he said. "Oh no, poor boy. Didn't you know nothing can hurt us? That's the Covenant for you. A demon won't allow its totem do us any harm."

The Prince jumped to his feet, shook his arm and a black Kanchak knife slipped out of his sleeve straight into his hand. The Prince raised his knife.

"You had your chance," he said, and attacked Gabriel with a wide slash. The boy jumped back, escaping the blow, but tripped and fell on his back.

"Freeze!" shouted Beatrice, leaning out of one of the three police cruisers dashing across the Old Port in their direction, lights flashing and sirens wailing.

She shot at the Prince, but the bullet missed.

"All guns, quiet! Stop the cruisers!" the Prince screamed at the approaching cars, and they stopped with a screech, while the second Prince shook his arm and a long, fiery whip unrolled in his hand with a hiss and a billow of smoke. "Kill the boy!" he screamed to his friend.

Beatrice tried to shoot again, but this time her gun didn't work at all.

The Prince raised his fiery whip, and with a roar of the old engine, Gabriel's mother's car drove between them, protecting Gabriel from the blow, as the whip hit its roof, leaving a smoking dent in the metal.

"I'm sorry, don't hurt me!" cried Pierre, the demon of the car. "Gabriel!"

Gabriel opened the door and jumped into the car, which started with a squeal of tires. But didn't even make fifty feet before the Prince raised his hand: "Stop the car!" and the car stopped.

"No! Keep going!" cried Gabriel in the back seat, making the Sign of the Covenant.

"No! They'll kill me!" Pierre shouted, covering his face with his hands.

The doors of the other police cars opened, and out jumped six officers, armed with batons, and four police dogs, as many as Beatrice could collect in such a short amount of time.

Beatrice holstered her gun and grabbed a nightstick from the car door.

"Release the dogs!" she cried, and as the officers removed their collars, the dogs rushed forward and stopped several yards in front of the Princes, barking and growling.

The policemen followed the dogs, their batons raised high, ready to strike. Beatrice walked with them, clutching her nightstick tightly, her eyes darting around the square to assess the situation.

"Drop your weapons!" cried one officer.

A Prince swished his whip in the air in one big sweep and hit the cop across the face. The fiery rope hissed on contact with skin; the cop cried out with pain and dropped to his knees, holding a smoking, black wound in his face. The whip whistled just millimeters from Beatrice's head, she jumped back at the last moment.

One of the dogs jumped up to the Prince and bit into his hand holding the whip. The Prince yelled with pain and the other one hit the dog in the neck with his black Kanchak knife, killing the animal on the spot.

"Get them!" Beatrice screamed and stormed at the Princes,

dealing a blow with her baton. She hit one of them in the head, he cried and bent in half, while the other one punched Beatrice in her chin, knocking her down.

At this moment, Gabriel opened the car door with one desperate kick and dashed across the waterfront. He jumped and pulled himself onto a container the size of a train car, still tied with chains to an enormous crane.

"Crane, up!" he shouted, making the Sign. The motors roared to life and he had to grab the chains not to fall off, as the crane pulled the container up in the air, high over the Old Jose's. "Now, turn! Over the water!"

The Princes noticed him and ran towards him.

"Stop!" one of the Princes roared and the crane stopped. "Pull him down!"

Gabriel dashed across the lowering, tilting container, and took a wild leap, the air whistling in his ears, and splashed legs-first into the metallic water of the harbor.

Cold water covered him as he went deep down with a cascade of air bubbles. Underwater, he swam as fast as he could, panicking, along the harbor line, trying to get as far away from the Princes as possible. His lungs burned; he had to get some air.

With several strong strokes, he pushed himself up to the surface, where he heard screams and noise, and noticed something that looked like an exit of a sewer pipe in the waterfront, with a diameter large enough for him to climb through, but it was closed off with a grating.

He grabbed the slimy, algae-covered bars and pulled, but it didn't budge. Shivering from cold, he noticed hinges on the side and a lock.

"Open up!" he hissed fervently, making the Sign.

The lock squeaked, some mechanism turned, and it let go.

He climbed into the pipe and shut the grating behind him. "Now, lock again!"

He made the Sign of the Covenant to the demon of the grating, the soaking wet hobo with green seaweed in his beard and the stinking breath.

"I'm a Seer and Ombudsman, and by the Covenant you should not open to anyone. And you will be quiet and not answer any questions about me! Understood?!"

The hobo nodded.

"Where's that pipe going? Is there another exit I can squeeze through?"

"It's just a rain drainage system. At the gate of the port is another manhole," murmured the hobo.

Gabriel nodded and, on all fours, crawled through the stinking sewage water pipe against the flow. It soon got dark, with him obscuring what little light came from behind him, but he saw another circle of light in the distance and began pushing towards it, hoping it was the manhole the demon told him about.

He feared he was going to get stuck. He could hear only his own heartbeat and the echoing dripping of the dirty water.

18

———

FOREVER TAINTED

Beatrice found herself paralyzed with fear at the sight of the carnage in the Old Port. The Princes turned to the cops and their dogs, one attacking with the whip, the other with the weird knife.

A knife stabbing from underneath and slipping into a skull in an explosion of red, the concrete of the harbor splattered with puddles of blood. A fiery whip cracking through the air, setting a dog's fur ablaze, beating a human body into a smoking, carbonized pulp. The screams of the men and whines of the animals.

She saw Delancey still sitting there at the white plastic chair, staring like an idiot into his cup of coffee amid the massacre.

She cursed him aloud, ducked and ran up to him, then grabbed him by the hand and tried to pull him. He didn't budge. He just stared at her with lack of understanding in his stupefied eyes.

"Andrew, run!" she screamed in his face and pulled him so strongly he fell off the chair. She kept pulling him between the deserted warehouses. He allowed himself to be dragged along, a frozen expression on his face, like a robot.

"We need to call for backup," she cried to him as soon as they hid behind a large warehouse.

He nodded with the same detached expression, like somebody having an out-of-body experience.

"It's Lubonsky!" she shouted into her phone. "We need backup. All SWAT teams ASAP at the Old Port! And ambulances! There are officers down!"

"Confirmed. Sending backup," the operator replied.

She disconnected and looked behind, through the narrow road between two warehouses, leading back to the harbor. It was quiet. Just the hum of the ocean and the cries of seagulls.

She reached back for her gun and looked at it dubiously, moving back the slide and reloading. It appeared to be functioning normally, but who knows what would happen if she tried to fire it at the two men in white. What she had seen was enough to fill her with dread at the thought of drawing their attention.

She moved Delancey to hide behind a shell of a motorboat leaning against the wall of the warehouse.

"What's wrong with you? Andrew?" she whispered to him. "Can you talk?"

"Yes," he answered with a bland voice.

"What's going on? What did they do to you? Gabriel called me before I called you this morning. He said you acted strange, and when I called you and heard your voice, I knew you weren't yourself. Are you on something?"

He lowered his eyes. She looked back to the harbor.

"God, I hope he's made it. Did you see him jump into the water? From that height? Hope he's fine... " She checked back to Delancey. He looked at her with a very sad expression on his face. "We need to see. We dragged him into this. We asked him to help with this case. It's on us. Andrew? I'm going."

She thought for a split second, hid her gun in her holster,

and reached to another holster on her belt and pulled out a combat knife with serrated blade.

She stole to the opening, keeping close to the wall of the warehouse, holding the knife so tightly her knuckles went white, and she carefully peeked behind the corner.

There was no trace of the Princes. It was still.

The bodies of policemen and dogs lay on the ground, their blood seeping into the cracked concrete of the old harbor. It was such a painful sight: she'd led them into this. Two of them she knew personally. They had families.

She scanned the shore for cover, and chose a place between the base of the port crane and an old rescue boat. She sprinted across the harbor and dived for the cover. She checked out the water below. Just waves, no trace of Gabriel.

She heard a distant rattling and looked up. The first SWAT chopper was approaching the Old Port. As it got closer, she saw a sniper in the door, inspecting the area through the scope of his rifle. She felt a vibration in her pocket as her phone rang.

"Agent Lubonsky? Delta-7. Take cover. We're checking the perimeter."

"Take a look at the water!" she said. "There was a teenage boy in the water. We need to make sure he's fine."

In the old lady's apartment, his clothes and hair still wet, breathing hard from running upstairs from a car he'd stolen at the port's parking lot, he quickly put his things into the old backpack and cargo pockets.

Maurice sat on the sofa and watched him calmly with his flame-colored eyes from under the brim of his hat.

"We need to take Matt from the orphanage and go hide somewhere they can't find us," Gabriel told him. "Like, I was thinking, the forest, right? That's how Ricko was hiding. Just nature around. No demon to tell them where I am."

"Well, we did find Ricko, didn't we?" Maurice answered.

"I traced him to the forest through the subway, and later Delancey found out about the construction site. But I won't be using a construction site. We'll ... we'll live in the trees ... or build something from branches. Even if they conjure up drones, they won't spot us through the trees. It will be fine."

"And what are you two going to eat?"

"I will get something right now, from the store."

"How long will that last?"

"Damn it, so I will hunt!"

"Can you hunt?"

Gabriel didn't answer, so Maurice continued: "Because I was thinking, did you consider the ocean?"

Gabriel looked at Maurice with surprise. "I thought you didn't like water."

"I hate water. But the ocean is big and no demons there neither."

"And what are we going to eat there?" Gabriel asked.

"Fish?" came the answer.

"We can eat game in the forest too. And look, it's easier to spot something on the open water. Nothing there to hide you."

"If you're on a boat? Are they going to check all the boats they see on the ocean?"

"They can send drones, and the drones will ask the boats."

"I just don't know how long you can live in a forest. Matt still isn't very healthy."

"There's no good option! Okay? None!" Gabriel threw the backpack on the floor and looked through the window at the street.

Then his phone rang. Beatrice.

"Gabriel! Finally, thank God. Are you okay?"

"I'm happy to hear you're alive, Agent," Gabriel said.

"Listen, we need to decide what to do now."

"Did you get them?"

"No. And, Gabriel ... they killed all the policemen and their dogs. Me and Delancey are fine."

"Is Agent Delancey with you?"

"Yes, but ... he's not in a position to speak."

"Ask him if he told the Princes about Matt and the orphanage."

"Gabriel..."

"Please, ask him."

There was a moment of silence, and then she simply said: "He did."

Gabriel stood there for a moment with the phone at his ear. Then, he killed the call.

"Gabriel? Hello?" Driving with her free hand, Beatrice looked at her phone and saw he had disconnected. She threw the phone aside and looked at Delancey, sitting next to her, looking idly through the windshield.

"Andrew, please, say something. He's fine. You made a bad judgement in a bad state of mind. Now, we have to concentrate on getting those fuckers."

Delancey nodded, so she looked back to the road. They were driving down the freeway from the Old Port. They drove onto an overpass.

She heard the alert beeping from Delancey's seatbelt getting unfastened, and before she even turned to him in surprise, he opened the door and slid out of the car.

His body hit one of the streetlights on the overpass at full speed and collapsed like a ragdoll.

She slammed on the brakes, the car squealed and stopped, and a semi-truck crashed into her from behind. Her head flew forward and hit the airbag.

Wiping the blood running from her nose, Beatrice undid her seatbelt, jerked the doorhandle, and pushed the door with all her might. She half-dropped, half got out of her wrecked car. She fell on her knees as for some reason, shock probably, her legs refused to carry her weight. The cars stopped in front and behind her, people running out, calling for help.

She got to her feet and, leaning on the hood, went around the car, leaned on the overpass barrier and continued toward Delancey. He lay there by the streetlight, huddled like an embryo. He opened his eyes as she knelt next to him and felt his neck for a pulse. His stare was penetrating and crystal clear.

"I'm not a man," he whispered.

"What is it?" she said with difficulty, swallowed, and crouched next to him. She was too weak to keep standing. "What you're saying?"

He laughed silently, his teeth red with fresh, bright blood.

"I brought him for them to slaughter. I took a drug... made of..."

"And now are you going to regret, or are you going to try and fix what you've done?" she screamed at him. People gathering around them were afraid to come closer. "What did you teach us? What were you fucking teaching us all that time? 'We are called upon to be strong. You won't escape that. You can't hide. It will keep coming at you until you're strong.' Your words, Andrew!"

"I can't do it anymore," he whispered, shaking his head, and closed his eyes.

She heard the deafening siren of an ambulance blaring next to them, quick footsteps, and the warning cries of paramedics.

BEATRICE WAITED for him in the reception area of Central Military Hospital. Her exam had been short. A doctor had shone a small flashlight in her eyes, moved her head to the sides, and she'd demanded she be let go—she was fine. Now she sat in a plastic chair in a row of identical chairs, holding an icepack to the bridge of her nose, trying to reach Gabriel, but he wasn't answering his phone.

"Bee!" cried a familiar voice, and Linda, her girlfriend from Communications, ran into the waiting room. She embraced Beatrice and kissed her head. "Are you alright?"

"I am, until you strangle me!" Beatrice gently pushed her away and petted the short, blond hair on Linda's head. She liked to touch it.

At the same time, the door to the doctor's office opened and Delancey walked out on his own. The doctor stood behind him, visibly concerned.

"Well, nothing seems to be broken. Andy here seems to have more luck than brains," he said. "I told him we need to keep him under observation for the night, but you know your boss."

"I do," Beatrice smiled. "Thank you."

The doctor saluted and went back to his office, as Beatrice approached Delancey.

"Well? Ready to go home?"

"I need to take a leak first," he muttered under his breath.

"Of course."

He disappeared behind the bathroom door. Linda squeezed Beatrice's hand and smiled at her with reassurement.

Then they heard a terrible scream, an inhuman wail, from the bathroom.

Beatrice pushed the door, but it was bolted from inside; the lock displayed an "occupied" sign. She took a step back and kicked it with all power she had; the doorframe cracked and wood splinters flew. One more kick sent the door slamming open and she ran into the small bathroom.

Delancey stood at the basin, in front of a mirror which was smashed in the middle, and turned to her with a bloody cobweb of broken skin on his forehead, and she understood he'd smashed the mirror with his head.

"Andrew!"

"You see that?" he cried, and showed her his trembling hand, filled with a pool of blood dripping from his forehead. "Those kids' suffering is flowing in my veins!"

Two big nurses ran into the room and grabbed him, putting his hands behind his back as he kicked around and cursed them with bloody foam dripping from his mouth.

Beatrice stood there, hiding her face in her hands, crying.

CROWE SAT at a table playing chess on his laptop in the side room they'd arranged for his office at the orphanage. The administration of course went mad upon hearing the agents were going to set up a provisionary operational center there, but there was little they could do against an order signed by the prime minister herself. The several free beds they got at the orphanage were too short, designed obviously for kids, so Crowe stayed at the Savoy in the center and came to the orphanage every morning. He had it better than the cops outside, who had to sleep in their cruisers.

There was a knock at the door and he raised his head. One of his agents poked his head into the room.

"There's someone to see you," the agent said, looking as if he saw a ghost.

"Who is it?" Crowe frowned and stood up, closing his laptop.

The agent pushed the door open, revealing Gabriel, wearing his backpack, and hood off his head, his hands bandaged and face scarred from dog attack, staring calmly at the secret agent.

"Well?" Gabriel said. "You've been looking for me."

19

———

THE CONVOY

SUN REFLECTED off the roofs of armored cars going slowly in a convoy down the freeway T-40 to the north, among the fields of dark soil, with the forest lining up the horizon to both sides: the deep woods of Shirnov. Above them, two MI-17 helicopters scouted their way, looking for danger ahead and a tail behind.

In the middle car, behind bulletproof windows, in the back seat Gabriel huddled next to Matt, holding his hand. Opposite them sat Agent Crowe, with two agents behind him, driving the car and providing protection.

Behind their car rode a military truck with marines. Gabriel had caught a glimpse of them when they were getting in, the wide-armed men with crewcuts, submachine guns, and knives at their belts. The Princes had said things couldn't harm them, but there were so many weapons in here that it was hard to believe they had a fighting chance.

Inside the car, Crowe looked at Gabriel with a good-natured smile.

"So, is that true what they say you can do? All those tricks? Can you, like, make my telephone ring?"

Gabriel turned his eyes to Crowe and stared at him for a while.

"Maybe you should go to a circus if you want to see tricks," he said finally, and turned his stare back to the forest in the distance.

The farthest he ever got from the city was two weeks at a sea resort with his parents long before Matt was born. He remembered the white sands of the beach, the castles they built, the holes they dug. His dad was tall and lean, his hair cut very short, and he always closed one eye when he laughed. He taught Gabriel to swim but the ocean was so cold. Dad, he remembered, had a long scar running all across his back and had never told him what it was from.

Now, if he could trust Crowe's enthusiastic presentation, they were headed to a military base with a special school for them, and playgrounds and football fields for him and Matt to play in, and they would see tanks and fighter jets—who knows, maybe even take a ride in them. What he was interested in, though, was protection, and according to Crowe it was the safest place in the country. Gabriel also imagined that being in a military base could give him the access to secret databases. Perhaps he could find information about their father. He would ask the computers for their secret files. And Matt would have a father again.

When he and the orphanage director had entered the room where Matt and the other boys his age were having an origami course, his little brother had run up to him and thrown himself into his arms so fast, he'd smashed Gabriel's lower lip against his teeth. But the older brother had so many scars already that he didn't mind.

The director told Gabriel his brother had begun to talk a little, but he hadn't spoken so far since they left the orphanage, and he didn't want to push him in front of Crowe. There would come a time for that. For now they were just sitting next to each other, and he held his brother's little hand tight in his bandaged fingers.

They passed by a sign that read "Omelsen Pass," and he couldn't help but gasp in a sudden realization.

"Gabriel? What's that?" Maurice appeared next to Crowe. "Did you see something?"

"Birdflipper," Gabriel said, and the CAISA agent raised his eyebrows in surprise.

"Excuse me?" Crowe said, but Gabriel looked to the right of him, at a person he couldn't see.

"You remember 'Birdflipper?' The mysterious word Andrea's father asked me about?"

"Yes?"

"Are you talking to a demon now?" Crowe got excited and moved as far as he could away from the invisible entity.

"Remember that image of the sea and the piece of rock? That's the Birdflipper."

"What do you mean?" asked Maurice.

"I knew the rock seemed familiar. It was a little one-day excursion we went to with school like three years ago. To Omelsen Rock. That was Omelsen Rock on the image from the cameras at the Bays' home."

"But why Birdflipper?"

"'I don't want to go to the Birdflipper,' she said, right? To get our interest, Miss Carlyle told us the rock looked like a man who's looking up, and the locals supposedly called it the 'Stargazer,' but when we were there, nobody could see the shape of the man in the stupid old rock. But Martin noticed it looked rather like a hand giving you the finger. And that's why we called it the Birdflipper, see? It was such a little thing that lasted one day only and I forgot."

Gabriel noticed Matt's smile listening to the story, and it made his heart melt. He squeezed his hand and smiled too.

"Funny, eh?" he said. "Martin was funny. I will tell you many stories about him. He has a YouTube channel we can watch."

"I know," Matt said, and Gabriel bit his lips and his eyes grew misty as he heard his little brother speak for the first time after the kidnapping. "We watched some of it already."

"That's right. You remember." Gabriel ruffled Matt's hair.

Crowe gave them an even wider fake smile. He seemed a bit weirded out by the conversation with the invisible demon about the Birdflipper, but maintained his professional cool.

"Watch out! Stop!" they heard from outside, and the car suddenly jerked to a halt.

The smile disappeared from Gabriel's lips. He exchanged concerned stares with Maurice, as Crowe reached for his radio.

"It's Crowe!" he barked, pushing a button on his radio. "Why are we stopping?"

"There's ... an obstacle," a voice replied.

"What?"

"There's a bulldozer, blocking the road ahead on both lanes."

"A bulldozer? There wasn't supposed to be any construction here," Crowe snapped. "Is there any contact with the driver?"

"Just a moment, sir..."

They waited and you could hear only their quickened breathing in the vehicle.

"Sir..." the radio came in. "It appears there's no driver."

Gabriel watched Crowe, the nerves on his face and his clumsy moves as he pressed his face to the glass trying to see, and a terrible feeling began to grow up in his belly.

"The last time," he whispered.

"What?" Maurice asked.

"This is the last time I trust humans to protect me."

Crowe tried to invoke his calming smile.

"Easy, boy. We'll move the obstacle and continue on our journey. You have no reasons to worry."

"Go back to the city," Gabriel said.

"That's out of the question."

"I wasn't talking to you. Car, go back to the city!" Gabriel cried, and made the Sign of the Covenant.

The car backed up, smashing into the van behind them, then made a U-turn and sped back towards Los Maines, passing the other cars of the convoy.

"Make it stop! Immediately!" Crowe shouted, grabbing Gabriel by the shoulder.

"Seatbelt! Hold him in place!" Gabriel snapped, and Crowe could only gasp as his seatbelt pulled up tighter and squished him against the back seat.

"How's that for a trick, Agent Crowe?"

They were speeding past the convoy.

"Sir! The bulldozer is moving ... it's ramming into the first car, and going on!"

Gabriel saw another bulldozer at the end of the convoy, slowly going into the last armored car, pushing it despite the squealing handbrakes, ramming it into the car ahead. The choppers circled above the scene like disoriented dragonflies.

"Go through the field!" cried Gabriel.

Their car veered into the ground and drove past the bulldozer. They could see there was no driver in there too.

Then they heard something, some voice crying something, and their car stopped just behind the bulldozer.

"Go! Why are you stopping?!"

"They told me so. I must listen," the Car replied.

"And I'm telling you to go!"

"I'm sorry, Ombudsman."

"Who told you to stop? Where are they?"

There was a moment of silence.

"They're coming."

"Wait here!" Gabriel whispered to Matt, yanking at the door. But it was locked.

"Let me out!" he shouted, and the door let go.

He jumped out of the car. The agents and soldiers escaped as their vehicles were pushed closer and closer to each other, and then began to compress with ear piercing noise and explosions of headlights.

"Helicopters, full kamikaze mode!" he heard a voice say, distorted by a bullhorn, and finally he saw them. They were walking towards the convoy through the field, calmly, two tall men in white suits, their blond hair flowing in the wind. One held a bullhorn at his mouth, through which he ordered the vehicles.

The two army helicopters dived down and crashed into the armored vehicles, tearing off their roofs and colliding in two balls of fire and smoke.

"Open fire!" cried one officer.

The soldiers took position among the fire and smoke and opened fire at the incoming Princes.

The air filled with the crack and noise of machinegun fire, many guns shooting at the two white silhouettes approaching calmly across the field, but Gabriel could see the bullets hitting the earth in explosions of dirt as if the Princes were enclosed in some sort of protective bubble.

"Things made by men will not hurt them," he said. "Now I see that's true."

"Gabriel," said Maurice. "Let's escape while we still can."

Gabriel stick his head back into Crowe's car. The agent groaned under the pull of his seatbelt, red in the face. Matt cowered on the back seat.

"Agent Crowe," Gabriel said. "Take Matt and run to the city. I will stop them."

"No!" Crowe said. "You're not ordering me ... Auch!"

The belt pulled him so tight he couldn't catch his breath.

"I prefer you listen to me. The situation has outgrown your abilities," Gabriel hissed, and Crowe nodded his head desperately.

Gabriel knelt next to Matt.

"It didn't work. Don't worry about me. I will take care of them."

"How?" Matt said. "I'm afraid."

"Be brave. That's why we were put on Earth. To be strong. You know? That's the mission. Crowe!"

He pointed at Crowe's belt and shoes.

"Belt and shoes. Give the agent some pain if he decides to go anywhere else than the city and the orphanage."

"I won't!" pleaded Crowe, and Gabriel freed him from the seatbelt.

"Fantastic. Once there, call NBI Agents Andrew Delancey and Beatrice Lubonsky. Give Matt to them. Goodbye, Agent."

Gabriel gave Matt a quick hug.

"I will see you. I will never leave you. Right?"

Matt nodded his head.

"Yes."

"Run, then! Run!"

Crowe and Matt, ducking to hide behind the cars, ran back the road towards the city.

Gabriel looked at Maurice.

"And how are we going to stop them, exactly?" Maurice asked.

"I don't know."

Gabriel walked around the vehicle to the side of the road the Princes were approaching.

He felt Alyssa heavy in his pocket, but he knew there was no point in shooting.

On the lumps of black fertile soil on the open field, the military convoy burning behind him, with his hands in his pockets, Gabriel waited for the Princes to approach him.

They took their time, leisurely, smiling at the world around them.

20

BITTER ROAD

T**HE TWO** P**RINCES** stopped a dozen feet away from him.

"Boo," said one of them.

"Are you very much scared?" asked the other one. "Are you dripping poo out of your butt and pee out of your little baby dick, soiling his panties and pants? That's a question that interests me somewhat."

He didn't answer.

"I don't know why you chose to leave our little date at the port," the second Prince said. "It was fun."

"You are two disgusting creatures," Gabriel answered. "You pretend you're having fun but you're pathetic. Two grownup pieces of shit picking on a teenager."

"We just picked on the choice of this country's army," noticed one the Princes. "If I'm not mistaken, they're burning and crying in pain just behind you, if you'd care to take a look."

Gabriel turned to take a look. The soldiers and military police were taking cover behind the burning wrecks of their vehicles. He didn't want to look for too long and awaken the Princes' suspicions, but he managed to see Crowe and Matt's silhouettes running on the other side of the road towards the city.

"The toy soldiers are trying to call their headquarters and ask for backup," said a Prince. "All that because two nice gents like us went for a stroll in the fields."

The other Prince took a look at his golden watch.

"I hate to be blunt on such a nice meeting. But do you have a mask for us?" he asked Gabriel.

"I do."

"Splendid! Let's see it, then, and get it all over with."

"I don't have it with me."

A Prince groaned in exasperation.

"Now we have to torture you. Normally, I would be happy to. It's always interesting to look for a pain threshold in a human, finding out new, interesting variants of fun, but we are kind of pressed for time..."

"Who are you working for? What's this, some kind of organization?" Gabriel asked.

"I'm not sure you're in a position to ask us any more questions," laughed the lisping Prince. "I don't really like your confidence either. You don't seem to fully grasp that next to us you are a slug, a turd lying in the grass. Human beings don't converse with turds. Where's the mask?"

"You'll never find it."

"Shoelaces! Belt! Tighten up and let's see some pain in that boy," a Prince snapped.

"If you'd care to take a look, I don't wear shoelaces in my shoes," Gabriel answered. "Also, I wear no belt. Regarding my clothes, the most you can do is order my pants to unbutton so you can kiss my ass." The Princes stopped smiling, and that was the only thing that gave Gabriel a modicum of satisfaction. "And that's as close as you can come to knowing where the mask is. Because none of my clothes was with me when I was hiding it."

With a hiss and crackling of the air, a Prince unrolled a fiery whip into his hand. Gabriel didn't even see him take a swing, he just heard a snap, then terrible pain exploded in his right cheek.

He smelled his burning skin. He cried out and grabbed his face. Tears welled in his eyes.

"You fucking maggot," the Prince said, his beautiful face twisted with hatred. "You disposable animal. Where is the mask?"

"Feel the cut in your skin? Feel the burned flesh?" The other Prince licked his lips repeatedly. "You know it's just the beginning? You know you will be crying for your parents to help and nobody will come? Just us, just us and our small pleasures that will be the last thing you experience before death swallows you up. And we will try to prolong that time ... you wouldn't believe how long a human can be kept alive ... even when forced to eat his own brain ... from his open skull..."

The other prince bent in two, coughing with laughter.

"Remember?" he asked the other one. "Oh, you had to remind me. Now I will have a hard-on for the next hour."

They came closer. Gabriel fought the urge to take a step back, but managed to stay where he was.

"The mask, dear," a Prince hissed, leaning into his face. "Tell us where it is."

"It's nearby," Gabriel said. "But that's my deal. You will never find it without me."

"We won't?" they laughed. "Why are you so sure?"

"Because it's in the forest," Gabriel replied. "Where you have nothing to ask or guide you."

The Princes stopped smiling.

"You overplayed your hand, little friend," said one of them finally. "We don't need it so much so as to suffer humiliation from a snot like you."

"You chased us all the way from the city, smashed a military convoy, and crashed two helicopters," Gabriel answered quietly. "I don't think I overplayed my hand."

"Why wouldn't you just give it to us when we asked you?" a Prince asked. "So many people would be still alive if you did."

"Because you want to kill everyone connected to Ricko Boleani's case," Gabriel said. "You said so yourself."

One Prince looked at the other.

"Damn your long tongue," he said.

"I want you to make a promise," Gabriel said in a quivering voice. "That if I give you the mask, you will leave the city and never come back here again."

The Princes looked at each other. They seemed surprised and meditated on something.

Gabriel hoped they would take the bait. He remembered what Maurice had told him about Ricko Boleani, how psychopaths considered humans a lower species, thoughtless slime, and themselves infinitely smarter than their victims, and how that blind spot was their weakness.

"No," a Prince said finally, and Gabriel felt a cold vise of panic close on his heart. "We're not idiots. We're not making any oaths before we actually see the mask. Right?"

"Damn right," said the second Prince. "And you better hurry, because I'm growing hungry. And I like small body parts of little boys to nibble on."

"It's close by," Gabriel said. "I told you."

"Well? Let's go, then."

"Maybe we should take one of the cars," Gabriel said.

"Maybe not. How far is it?"

"Maybe ten minutes' ride."

A prince hit him with a fist in his forehead. Gabriel saw a flash, and fell back on his butt.

"You just happened to hide the mask ten minutes ride away from here?" The Prince sneered. "Just so happens your hiding place was along the way you were escaping with those jesters?"

"Just so happens!" shouted Gabriel through the tears of pain that appeared in his eyes even though he was trying to stop them. "Because it so happens I wanted to take it with me, on my way away from here."

They were silent, thinking, looking at each other.

"Kill me if you want," Gabriel said. "You will never find your precious mask. And whoever sent you will be delighted when you return empty-handed."

"Stand up and take us to the mask," a Prince said with menace. "And remember, we aren't somebody you can hide from. If you try a trick, we will go and take your little precious brother who thinks he's running away with the agent unnoticed, and we will make you eat his tiny baby dick."

The other Prince looked at the first one with shining eyes and licked his lips.

"Beautiful image," he whispered, and shivered from pleasure. "Like a rose inserted into a knife wound in a young girl's thigh. Like screwing someone into a hole you cut in their muscle. You're a poet."

Gabriel scrambled to his feet without a word, turned away from the Princes and started walking through the empty black field towards the distant wall of the coastal forest. The Princes walked behind him, under low hanging, leaden clouds in the kind of sky so huge you never see it from the inside of a city.

The Princes grew quiet when they entered the forest. Gabriel led them the best he could. He hoped he'd chosen the direction well.

He trudged on, tripping over roots, pushing through thorny bushes on the most difficult march of his life. Whether he would fail or succeed with his plan, he knew he would die either way. He hoped it would be quick. He didn't really care if there was an afterlife. The eternal void, the absence of pain, was better than this.

He stopped because the Princes saw berries they wanted to pick. They ate some of them and made a game of throwing the rest in his face one by one while he stood and waited for them to finish. He didn't even move his head to avoid the soft little projectiles.

He looked at the two men as the berries hit his face, wondering where the Princes were from. He couldn't make out any discernible accent in their speech. They looked like models and their bodies were lean and agile. He had usually only seen people like that in commercials. The Princes were like better versions of humans, with an empty hole in their heads where conscience or empathy should reside.

"Let's go," a Prince ordered.

And they continued their march west, where the ocean should be. The forest was stuffy and dark. The ground was soft and overgrown. Minutes passed.

From time to time, one of the Princes waved his fiery whip in the air and smacked Gabriel's back. His hoodie was in tatters. The scalded skin hurt more than the blows. He couldn't help it any longer; he was crying as he plodded on, with sneering bullies at his back.

"Come on," said one of them finally. "He lied to us. He has no idea where he's leading us. Let's kill him right now and continue looking in the city."

"We're here," Gabriel said and pointed to where the trees grew sparse and you could see the open sky. They heard the ocean and seagulls.

They walked out of the forest onto a grassy cliff rising high over the steely waves of the Pacific Ocean. To the right, they had Omelsen Rock, the Stargazer, the Birdflipper. And there was no one there.

He looked around with a sinking heart. He was wrong. All was lost. They were going to torture him to death on this rock, then go back to the city and do the same to his little brother.

"Well? Where the fuck is it?" asked a Prince.

He closed his eyes, lifted his face to the sky and called: "Andrea!"

Silence, only the hum of the waves.

"What?" a Prince asked. "Who are you calling?"

"Nobody," he said.

It was all over. He had failed. He had miscalculated.

Gabriel looked at the steely ocean roaring deep below Omelsen Rock, and a sudden hope of rescue came over him. He pushed himself forward and began to run, desperate to jump, not caring about what lay below.

He cried out in pain as a hissing, fiery blow cut his ankles and he fell to the ground.

The Prince rolled back his whip. The two walked up to him and stood over him as he knelt in the grass with his head hung low.

"Were you going to jump?" one of them asked.

Gabriel didn't answer. He closed his eyes. There was no reason to try and do anything anymore.

"Well," sighed a Prince. "We've been taken for a ride. Let's start working on him. This is a nice place for some mutilation. I bet in fifteen minutes he'll tell us everything he knows."

"You know, I think we have greatly overlooked the importance of knees in our former work," said the other twin. "I knocked my knee against a chair the other day and it hurt like hell. I remembered the spot. I would like to cut into little Gabriel's and see if he agrees it's a damn sensitive spot."

"Knees! Right on. I want to conduct an experiment as well. I wonder if it's possible to extract an eyeball so it doesn't break, you know? I dream of holding an eyeball in my hand, like this big marble... Oh, and, you know? I wonder ... if I managed to remove one of his eyes, but leave all the veins and stuff still connected to his brain, would he see in the direction I point the eye at? You know what I mean? I would take his eye, still connected, and point, like, to his own face, so he can see himself!"

"That's ingenious. But, you know? Let's give him some Koloton first, so he appreciates the experiments better. Where's that damn syringe ..."

Gabriel felt his body begin to shake uncontrollably in anticipation of the torture.

And he cried again, with desperation, as loud as he could, his voice breaking on the verge of weeping. "Andrea!"

"My name is Eden," answered a calm voice.

21

___

EDEN

THEY TURNED BACK to the forest.

Andrea, with her long hair loose and her hospital gown dirty and torn, stood there staring at them calmly.

"We are Ombudsmen," Gabriel said. "Me and the two of them. Kill us."

"What are you—?" A Prince turned to him with a sneer, but couldn't do anything more, as Andrea opened her mouth and said just one word.

"*Ahanari.*"

And nothing happened.

"Aha—what?" asked one Prince after a moment of surprise.

"Who's that little bitch? She has the mask?" the second one wanted to know.

Gabriel stared at Andrea with an open mouth, not sure what was going on.

A prince unrolled the fiery whip, cracked it in the air and moved towards Andrea.

First came the hum.

Then a cloud of swirling black dots flew out of the woods and moved towards them as Andrea just stood there undaunted and proud.

"The wild bees!" Gabriel heard Maurice's voice.

Gabriel dived to the ground and covered his head with his hood when the swarm fell down on them. He heard the screams of the Princes as the bees covered every inch of their bodies and started to pump venom from their stings into their muscles. They waved their arms and jumped around like epileptic puppets.

The bees covered his body as well. He felt their hairy bodies as they pushed under his hood and crawled into his sleeves and trousers. Soon he felt his face covered with busy legs, on his lips, his cheeks, his eyelids. He was ready to die and he knew it would be painful.

The Princes screamed. They howled.

And he realized the bees crawling all over his body hadn't stung him yet.

He carefully lifted his bee-covered face from the ground to look. Andrea stood with her arms slightly open, a swarm of bees circling her, forming a protective bubble.

The Princes were tearing fistfuls of bees from their swollen heads, tears streaming down their faces, twisted in agony of pain.

One of them managed to crouch and pick up the flaming whip hissing and twirling on the ground in billows of smoke. He grabbed the bees away from his eyes and waved the whip in front of his face, scaring away the insects, which lifted from him like a tingling curtain.

He moved the whip next to his twin, and as the fire scared off the bees he immediately turned to Andrea, ran and cracked the whip at her.

The fiery rope hit her on the shoulder, cutting open the hospital gown and leaving a red scar on her skin. She cried out and took a step back.

The Prince laughed and rose his whip to strike again, right as a powerful ball of fur hit him from the side. The first gray wolf jumped on him and knocked him to the ground. Then the whole pack followed the first from among the trees, their fangs bared and their maws wrinkled with rage, dashing at the two men in white.

One of the wolves, a thin, mangy beast with his maw half-eaten in some fight, stood in front of Gabriel, baring its fangs, staring at him with deadly threat in his wild eyes, and Gabriel knew he'd better not move.

So he just watched as four wolves attacked one of the Princes, who defended himself with his Kanchak knife. He killed one wolf, sticking his knife between the animal's shoulders, then cut the other one's throat open while the two other wolves behind bit into his legs and tore open his calves. He dropped to his knees while a flock of seagulls dived down and attacked his head; others scratched him with their talons. The Prince tried to chase them away, but a wolf jumped at him and felled him onto his back. As the Prince still tried to push him away, the wolf closed his powerful jaws on the man's face and tore it off. A fountain of blood erupted into the air and the wolf threw aside the flap of skin, complete with nose and eyebrows and eyelashes around the holes for eyes.

Meanwhile, thanks to his fiery whip, which he waved all around him so fast he seemed to be enclosed within a cage made of fire, the second Prince managed to hold his ground. The wolves and wild dogs and birds large and small surrounded him with snarls and cries and tried to push through, but one cut of the flaming whip made them move back.

The Prince cried out when he saw his twin's fate, his brother's corpse twitching on the grass with red mush in place of the smooth, proud face. He crouched and grabbed the Kanchak, still flailing the whip around with his other hand.

Screaming out expletives, the Prince moved steadily ahead, waving his whip around, towards Andrea, who was still standing there peacefully and staring at him.

He knelt on one knee and swung his whip around them, forming a circle of fire no wolf dared to cross.

For the first time she seemed afraid. She made an attempt to run out of the circle of fire, but he grabbed her arm and pulled her to the ground, then sat with his knees on her stomach, his one hand squishing her breast, pushing her to the ground, his other holding the shining black blade of the Kanchak knife at her throat. She held his knife-wielding arm with both hands, but he was much stronger and pushed down with no effort.

"I will fuck you in the hole I cut in your heart," he hissed. "I am a Prince among men, an ordained master of their creation, and nothing can hurt me—"

"And I am not a thing," said a voice behind them, and the Prince looked up and saw Gabriel, with his head covered in a hood, stepping through a wall of fire and throwing himself at him. Gabriel grabbed at the Prince's neck with his bandaged hands.

The Prince roared and managed to get to his feet with Gabriel hanging from his back, his arm locked around his throat and squeezing, squeezing, with all his strength. The Prince ran, trying to shake the young man off him. They passed the wall of fire, and the wolves got at his legs so he fell, and the cloud of birds descended upon them.

Gabriel had to turn his face away and shut his eyes from the flapping wings, as each and every bird wanted its turn at pecking, and he soon felt his strangling arm wet with blood, and the man under him was not moving on his own anymore, just being jerked to the sides by the furious animals.

He struggled to his feet. He could barely stand. His whole body hurt. The wolves at his feet were ripping the Prince's body to shreds, the ground strewn with pieces of flesh and white scraps of his elegant suit.

Gabriel looked up at Andrea, standing several feet away

from him, a white-gray curtain of seagulls and birds of the forest waving behind her like a huge sail in the sky.

The whip was no longer burning; it lay smoking on the grass, bereft of its power with the death of its owner.

Gabriel and Andrea stared into each other's eyes.

The wolves, sensing something, stopped devouring the human monsters. They raised their maws and looked at Gabriel with their scary, wild eyes.

Andrea made a small gesture with her left hand and the wolves one by one ran into the forest. And the bees flew to their hives. And the curtain of birds fragmented and they flew away.

Andrea approached him. He could see the torn hospital gown and a glistening scar on her shoulder.

"You didn't kill me," he said.

She moved her face closer and he could smell her musky hair, and she kissed him. Her lips were soft and warm.

When their lips parted, she looked him in the eyes, but they were still embracing, and he felt her pounding heartbeat and the warmth her body emanated.

"Take me," she said quietly.

She grabbed his hand and led him away from the place of the carnage, to the edge of the cliff where a lone oak tree spread its branches. With the ocean roaring below them, she lay on the grass. He lay on top of her and this time he kissed her.

Their kisses went from delicate to passionate and hungry, and he felt desire overcoming him, and they made love on Omelsen Rock, under the open sky turning into night.

Afterwards, they lay on her old blanket. Andrea kept her head on his chest as a pillow, and they looked at the constellations so clearly visible here, away from the city.

It was a night of crisis in the weather, alive with invisible currents; the warm wind came in waves from the great distances over the horizon. But there was no moon visible, only the stars.

At some point Gabriel looked to the forest and saw fireflies gracefully cruising low among the bushes.

"Why didn't you kill me, Andrea?" he asked.

She kept silent for a while. "You know," she answered finally, and he knew.

"You can talk to all of that?" He made a gesture with his head. "The grass, the trees? The animals? What is it like?"

"Scary. Beautiful. And it changes everything," she replied.

They lay there, together, listening to the cracking of the waves, wrapped in the warm wind, under the satellites on their errant ways, under wandering stars. Civilization was somewhere faraway, sending its invisible signals through the air, recognizable only by a pale-yellow aura on the horizon—the downtown of Los Maines.

For them nothing existed apart from their own private empire stolen from the night, a nest with enough space only for two souls.

Gabriel awoke with the first dew and shivered with cold. But he didn't want to stand up and bring it all to an end. He looked down at Andrea's rich chestnut hair spread across his chest, and her long-fingered hand closed on his right shoulder. He reached and stroked her firm, young arm, marveling that it was at all possible—him, the school's timid wallflower, and the most pretty and popular girl from the gymnastics team—and that he could touch her, and that only several hours earlier they'd had sex.

He reached for the blanket and covered her back.

She sat up and looked at him.

"Good morning," he said with a smile.

"You have to go," she said, and her voice sounded hollow.

"And you? You want to stay here?"

She stood up, the blanket falling off her. She was suddenly distant.

What had happened?

"You don't understand anything."

"Then tell me."

"I don't want to stay here. I *will* stay here. This is what I am. The Watcher on the Rock."

"I want to stay here with you."

"No."

"But why?"

"Because I made a great mistake and I will not repeat it. Don't ever come back here. Don't even enter a forest, because a bird will tell a bird and a tree will tell a tree and I will come for you. And you will not survive the third time."

"Why do you want to hurt me?"

She stared at him, tears slowly welling in her eyes, until she said bitterly:

"Because you will kill the world."

"I will kill the world? I have no intention of—"

"Go now!" she screamed at him, stomping her foot. "*Ahanari!*"

With her face distorted from crying, she turned away from him and ran towards the top of Omelsen Rock. He heard something behind him.

The wolves were here, their fangs bared. They separated him from Andrea.

He took one last look at her, a lonely girl standing tall on the top of the cliff over the ocean, and turned back and started on his way towards the city.

THE PAIN, whose first inklings appeared once Andrea woke from the night spent in Gabriel's arms, filled her skull. She grabbed her head and dropped to her knees, pressed her face into the cold rock and whispered: "I'm sorry, I'm sorry."

It hurt so much and she felt so bad.

"Eden," she heard the voice of the Horned One. "Did you betray us?"

"No. No!"

"You lay with an Ombudsman," the voice continued. "Instead of killing him, you betrayed us."

"I couldn't do it!" she cried into the rock. "It was too difficult."

"You have feelings for him."

"No."

"We understand them. They are what sets life in motion and allows life to survive. But your heart chose wrongly. It chose a death bringer."

"I know."

"You could have ended it all. We could be safe here and now. But you chose your feelings for the boy."

"I want to go back to the meadow. I want to dream in the flower again. Please take me there."

"The meadow lies in the land of dreams, Eden, and this is the reality where our doom is coming. Without the dream, there will be no reality, but without reality there will be no one left to dream. Do you understand?"

"I want to return to the meadow."

"You will return to the meadow. But first you have to fulfill your role as the Watcher on the Rock. You have to save us from the Rising Star that heralds total destruction to the world of things and the world of dreams. You failed to stop it when you had a chance. The next chance will be the last one. For you, for us, for life itself."

The Horned One went away in the breeze. Andrea raised her face, wet with tears, and stared at the ocean, unchanging, undulating, although unclear—dead or alive.

"Eden," she heard a coarse voice say.

She turned her head and saw the gray wolf with the torn

maw. It held a dead rabbit in its fangs. It lowered its head and put the rabbit on the ground.

"Eat," the wolf said.

She felt revulsion ... and wild hunger at the same time. She grabbed the little furry body, still warm with the life deserting its veins, tore open the skin punctured by the wolf's fangs, and bit into the hot meat and delicious fat.

"I am Growl," the wolf said. "I run across the forest at night in the ecstasy of the hunt, where blessed, joyous rage and urges to kill fills my body. Weaker ones know me as the danger in the dark, and they choose to hide or surrender, as they know the cycle of life. A strange voice appeared in my den one night and ordained me to be Eden's protector, as even the bears fear me. I will care for you and provide for you. You need just call. Hah! Never did I suspect I would be a dog to a human. But you are Eden. Eat, Eden, and continue your watch. I go to sleep, for the day is already strong."

She swallowed a bite and nodded at the wolf. "You can go, Growl," she said. "Thank you for the food."

The wolf went back to the forest. Andrea sat and ate whatever she could bite off the rabbit's bones. She wiped the blood off her chin and stood, turning back to the ocean. She stood on the cliff, on the same wind that brought the waves crashing below her, standing her duty as the Watcher on the Rock.

22

DREAM OF FATHER

"You did it," Matt whispered. "I was so worried. I couldn't sleep the whole night."

They stood on the two separated sides of the chain-link fence. Matt had his fingers through the holes and Gabriel held them.

"Well, the wolves helped," he said.

"But you could have died. You didn't know she wasn't going to kill you."

"What's important is we're safe now, Matt. They can't hurt us anymore."

Gabriel thought for a while, staring at his one-eyed brother.

"Crowe's here?" he asked.

"He dropped me here yesterday, making several phone calls at once," Matt replied. "Giving reports and orders, about the Princes mostly. Meeting the other men who escaped from the convoy. He seemed to be very angry and scared by what happened."

"Yeah, I can understand. He saw more tricks than he could wish for."

"But I don't think he gave up on you. You must be careful. If he finds out you're alive, he'll want to get you."

"Don't worry about me. You know what I'm going to do? I'm going to find Dad, so he can take you from here."

Matt looked at him in disbelief. "You know where he is?"

"No. But I'm going to find out. It's not so difficult for me now."

Matt was silent for a second. He seemed agitated with the prospect.

"Do you remember him well?" he asked. "What is he like?"

"He's big, and strong. And likes to joke and play," Gabriel said. "You'll see for yourself."

"But when?"

"As soon as possible."

Matt thought some more, staring at his feet with a frown.

"Take me from here," he said finally. "Let's look for him together."

"You don't like it here? The boys pick on you?"

"No, it's okay. At nights I have bad dreams, but I tell myself they're just dreams and I'm not afraid."

"So why do you want to leave?"

"I just want to be with you."

"But this is no life for a little boy, Matt, you know? You have to play with other boys and you have to go to classes. I ... I don't want you to be like me."

"Why?"

"Matt?" they heard someone calling.

Matt's caregiver stood on the stairs to the orphanage, looking for him.

"It's Julianna," Matt said.

"Go," whispered Gabriel.

Matt nodded. They squeezed each other's fingers goodbye. Matt turned away from him and ran to the woman.

· · ·

GABRIEL WENT to the Chinese restaurant on the corner. The cook greeted him warmly as a familiar face and that embarrassed him. Displays of familiarity made him self-conscious. He preferred his ordering and shopping to be fast and anonymous.

He ordered fried rice with shrimp.

"Take out?" the cook asked him, and without waiting for the reply he reached for a paper bag.

"Actually..." He made a quick decision. He didn't have to stay by the orphanage every moment anymore. "No, I'll eat here."

He took his plate and chopsticks and went outside to one of the three small tables on the sidewalk.

"Li, call Agent Delancey," he said, chewing the first bite and putting his phone next to the plate.

"Again?" Li asked, and added after a while. "Still doesn't answer. I just get a busy signal. No voicemail, no nothing."

"Try Agent Lubonsky."

"Hi, Gabriel. I was losing hope of ever hearing from you again," Beatrice said.

"Yeah, I'm hard to get rid of," he smiled. "Listen, I tried to get hold of Agent Delancey..."

Her voice became hesitant and sad. "Yes, he ... he's unavailable, Gabe."

"What happened?"

"Well ... it's hard for him to come to terms with his mistake. They had to, well, tranquilize him. He's at a closed clinic right now, and when he gets his bearings, well, it's rehab for him."

"Rehab? Really, he agreed to go?"

"He was given a simple choice. Job or juice. Either he goes clean or he's fired."

Gabriel sighed. "How is he?"

"Sedated."

"I would like to visit him. Tell him I'm not angry at him. I understand. Those weren't humans we were fighting. There was a lot of pressure."

"I think that would mean a lot to him. I just don't really think he'd understand what you're saying right now. When I said sedated, I meant it. At least he's in his favorite state."

"Beatrice, before all that happened, I asked him to do a thing for me. And maybe you could help."

"Won't hurt to ask."

He switched off the speaker and put the phone to his ear.

"I asked him to find my father for me," he said. "Michael West. He did some government work. Agent Delancey said there was nothing on him in regular files, but he could dig deeper. I assume there was no time."

"I'll call you when I have something."

"Thank you, Beatrice."

After he finished eating, Gabriel walked down the street to the building where the old lady's apartment was. He stopped in the street, staring at its glum windows and dusty curtains. He remembered the smell of mothballs and the old sofa.

He turned to his mother's car.

"Pierre?"

"Yes, kiddo?"

"What's the best hotel in the city?"

"My expertise in such places is that the more confident you act, the fewer suspicions you awake," whispered Maurice when Gabriel set his foot on the marble steps of the Massini Hotel. "I believe you look just right: there's a thin line between the extravagance of the rich and the shabbiness of cheap garments. Just look straight ahead and walk on with confidence."

"Well, I'm confident. What can they do to me? Throw me out?" said Gabriel, passing a doorman in black attire who held the door open for him.

In the lobby, everything seemed to shine, from chandeliers

to the humming, illuminated fountain, to the black marble floors.

"Can I help you?" asked a receptionist behind a desk, looking at him as if he were an alien.

Gabriel walked up to the desk and took a look at the receptionist's computer.

"Come out," he said.

"Excuse me?" the receptionist asked.

Next to him, another receptionist appeared, the demon of his computer, differing only in the bluish color of his skin.

"I have a fully paid reservation here, for a week, in your best unoccupied apartment," Gabriel said, and made the Sign of the Covenant.

"Yes, Ombudsman," said the demon receptionist, while the human receptionist made a face as if he'd bit into a lemon.

"And ... may I have your name, young sir?"

"Sure. I'm ... Martini Bianco."

The receptionist typed his name into the system, with his smirk showing that he realized it was a prank. But then his smile disappeared as the computer confirmed the reservation.

"Certainly, sir. I'm sorry, sir." The receptionist's smile now reached from one ear to the other. "Do you need help with your baggage?"

Gabriel patted his backpack.

"Oh, no. I'm fine."

"Your suite is waiting for you, of course. Here's the card." The receptionist gave him a small envelope. "Jimi, please take Mr. Bianco to his suite."

"I'm sure I'll find it," Gabriel said quickly. He wasn't used to people being so nice to him and helpful. It made him nervous.

"Certainly. It's floor twenty."

"And the room number is...?" Gabriel looked at the envelope with the keycard, but it was blank.

"Well … there's only your suite on that floor. Is that fine with you?"

"I guess I can live with that!" Gabriel said cheerfully. "Thank you, my good man."

THE ELEVATOR PLAYED A DISCREET SONG, and he didn't really feel it moving. Suddenly he heard a soft gong and a number twenty came on the screen above the elevator door, but it didn't open.

"I think you need to use the card now," Maurice said.

"Oh." Gabriel put the card to the reader next to the door.

The door opened into a huge, breathtaking room. The first thing he noticed was the panorama of the city below, stretching out for miles to the ocean. The apartment had transparent walls, from the floor up to the very ceiling. There was a white Steinway piano too, with a golden stool, a crazy puffy sofa by a gigantic TV screen, a drink station, and a Jacuzzi in the corner. There were whole hills of fresh flowers, and fruit on the tables. In the second room, Gabriel noticed a pool table.

The bathroom was amazing as well, bigger than his old apartment. The washbasins were flat plates of transparent glass, and there was no showerhead, just water dropping down like tropical rain from the ceiling of a small rocky cave.

"I think I found my headquarters," Gabriel said, coming back into the main room and taking off his sneakers so as not to spoil the fluffy carpet. "Look, the curtains are automatic!" He pressed a button on a remote and the curtains began to close all along the room on their own. "I have to show Matt this place!"

"I could get used to this life!" said Li, spreading his legs on the sofa and crossing his hands behind his head.

"Eh, it's too eclectic. No real style, cheap glamour," grumbled Maurice, but quickly found himself a nice spot in front of a futuristic fireplace where the flames moved inside a glass tube. "I expected something more subdued from Massini."

"I could sleep on this carpet and it would be comfier than the sofa at the old lady's place," said Gabriel happily. "Do you think I can drink those?"

"I thought you said it's fully paid, so…" Maurice sneered.

"Ah come on. They're so rich nobody will notice my spending a night here. I'm not going to feel guilty about it."

"Who mentioned guilty?"

"Nobody. Cheers!" Gabriel took a chilled bottle of beer from a transparent fridge behind the drink station, saluted his demon companions, and drank some. He sat on the futon and admired the view from his luxury suite.

"Francis Bay calling," Li said. "Again."

"Drop him," sighed Gabriel. "How can I explain to him his daughter decided to live on a rock and sets wolves on people who have the bad idea to disturb her."

"I really wonder what she's doing up there. What's the whole agenda?" Maurice said, staring into the fire.

"Go and ask her," Gabriel said.

"Well, there was at least ONE of us who found her company not totally unpleasant," Li said, and he and Maurice laughed.

"Shut up, you two."

Li frowned.

"Now it's agent Lubonsky calling."

"Pick up!" Gabriel stood up from the futon. "Hello?"

"Hi, Gabriel … I'm calling about your father," Beatrice said. "I'm … well, it's a strange case. We didn't have him in the common database, so I searched the mainframe for any records, and it seems we did have a file on him. A paper one, kept in an archive at Rosovo Main Bureau. The thing is, around one year ago, there was an accident and the archive burned."

Gabriel and Maurice exchanged looks.

"There's no hope, then?" Gabriel asked with a sinking feeling.

Beatrice sighed.

"Here's the thing. Seems there's no harm as your father's nowhere to be found, and I think you deserve to know, but, well, legally I shouldn't be telling you this, right?"

"Please, Beatrice ... please, tell me."

"If your father's file was at Rosovo Archive, it means he was in active service at either counterintelligence, CAISA, or us. Since he wasn't us, it leaves the two. But our reach doesn't extend to their archives."

"I see," Gabriel said. "Thank you, Beatrice."

"And remember. I didn't tell you any of this. Understood?"

After the call, Gabriel and Maurice looked at each other for some time, thinking.

"Seems your dad was a spy," Maurice said.

"Or a spy hunter. That's what counterintelligence means, correct?"

"Of course, we don't know if he worked in the field. Could have been just an office worker..."

"And that's why he disappeared for weeks on end?" Gabriel interrupted and shook his head. "I have to get to the bottom of this."

"Well, we know someone from CAISA."

"Crowe."

Maurice nodded and closed one eye in a clever grimace.

"And I happen to have an idea how we can use him."

After they discussed their plan, Gabriel took a long, hot shower. It felt so good. He watched as water cleaned the wounds, scars, scabs, and mud on his arms, legs, and torso. He closed his eyes in the warm rain, leaned against the wall and half-slept, thinking of Andrea and her naked body.

When he noticed he was dozing off, he shook his head, turned off the water and wiped himself with one of the lush, thick towels. Without even caring to put on anything, he walked through the dark to the bedroom adjacent to the main room, jumped on the soft royal bed, slipped under the covers, and fell asleep even before he put his head on the pillow.

His father's terrified face in the metal locker. The tube in his mouth, drowning his screams. The hum of the engines, the vibrations.

Gabriel screamed and sat up in his bed. He was breathing heavily and his hair was wet with sweat. He saw a line of gray light under the heavy curtains covering the windows. A new day was dawning.

23

STORIES FROM THE SEA

CROWE WALKED out of the Savoy wearing his impeccable gray suit. He was freshly shaved, smelled of cologne, and carried a paper cup of coffee. He looked around for the valet.

"Hello, Agent," said a familiar voice.

Crowe turned and saw Gabriel standing just behind him, with his hands in his pockets and a big smile on his scarred face.

"Whoa. If it isn't Gabriel West. Talk about a surprise," Crowe boomed with his manliest voice. He never allowed himself to look surprised. "I'm so happy to see you."

Gabriel smiled.

"Li, call him."

"What?" Crowe frowned, and at the same time his phone started ringing. He moved the coffee to his other hand and fished his phone out of his jacket and stared at the screen. "You're calling me?"

"Phone, listen to Maurice," Gabriel said, and made the Sign of the Covenant.

"Excuse me?" Crowe smiled with pretend goofiness, but his eyes betrayed his intense brainwork. "I'm not sure I understand."

"How is the Savoy, Agent Crowe? I find it a bit low-class myself," Gabriel said.

"Gabriel." Agent Crowe rejected the call and put his phone back in his pocket. "I see you're in a funny mood. And I'm delighted to see you alive. Can we please stop with the jokes and sit down somewhere to talk? We've been through a lot!"

"What do you want to talk about, Agent Crowe?"

"About the great things we could do together? Things where you can do something important, like helping your country, or saving innocent people from dying? Does that sound like something worthwhile?"

"Uh-uh" Gabriel shook his head. "Sounds boring."

Crowe clenched his jaw as the inborn aggression took over, but then his strong will and training helped him to calm down and smile again.

"You're right. Sorry for being so cheesy. You caught me. We will pay you, okay? Really big sums. Comfortable life for you and your brother."

Gabriel suddenly turned his head, as if listening to someone else, then smiled and nodded at Crowe.

"Agent Crowe, I think it's time we parted ways. Enjoy your coffee."

"No, no, no, wait, please..."

"Laces! Give me five minutes' handicap," Gabriel said, making a sign with his left hand, and broke into a run, pushing through the morning crowd at Savoy plaza, while Crowe made a few steps chasing him, dropped his coffee, and cried with sudden pain, falling to his knees when the shoelaces of his fine leather Oxford shoes squeezed his feet.

GABRIEL JUMPED on a bus at the last moment before the doors closed, went to the back where there were no people, and looked through the back window. Satisfied he wasn't followed, he sat down and called Maurice out. He didn't remember when he last saw the demon so excited.

"Okay, this is huge." Maurice pushed his hat to the back of his head. "I don't even know where to start. You won't believe this."

"Start at the beginning! Come on."

"As I expected, Crowe's phone had clearance, and an app with access to the CAISA database. I told him to give me all he had on your father. Turns out, yes, he was a CAISA agent."

Gabriel slammed the seat with his fist from excitement.

"Go on!"

"When you last saw him, he was sent on a mission to Russia to infiltrate their covert war submarines program. You know, the kind that goes underwater and fires a number of nuclear missiles that can wipe out a whole city?"

"Yes, yes, and then?"

"The last report they had from him was five years ago, when he joined the crew of one submarine called a Typhoon. Here his reports end. CAISA hadn't heard of him since."

"I can't believe Mom didn't tell me any of this. She must've known!"

"Well, I wouldn't be so sure she knew. It's secret services. They can't tell many things to their own families."

Gabriel looked out the window. The day was dark and cloudy. Crowds on the sidewalks passed by shop displays of international clothing brands. Thoughts raced in his head.

"Well, what now, then?" he said finally. "How can I go looking for a lost Russian submarine?"

"So ... here's when it gets weird," said Maurice. "Maybe it's a stretch, but the coincidence is uncanny. I just have to ask you to keep an open mind. Listen ... there are urban legends, right? Tales of an alligator in the sewers, or a haunted laundromat, whatever. Things that demons who are bored tell each other, from one newspaper carried by the wind to a discarded old telephone to traffic lights. We tell ourselves what we heard, you know about it—you saw me many times listening to the city voices in the evenings."

"Get to the point," Gabriel interrupted. "Maurice, say it already."

"I've heard rumors of a submarine deep down on the bottom of Los Maines Bay."

It took Gabriel a while to even react.

"What?"

"As I said—maybe a crazy rumor."

"What are the chances?"

"Chances. Or fate. Or who knows what."

"It could explain my dreams." Gabriel felt like he had fever. "I mean, stranger things have happened to me, right?"

"I know."

"On the bottom of the bay ... but, like, stuck? Or operational? If it's sunk, that would mean he's—"

"I don't know the details. I just heard there's a lost submarine there that people don't know of. Never paid it much thought. But, you know ... I heard they can live for years, independent of the surface world. They have food, water, air. They're nuclear powered."

Gabriel stared at him with open mouth and kept nodding.

"Yes. Yes. How do we go about finding it? Do you remember who told you about it?"

"I lived for years in my playground, remember? I guess it was a magazine some mom read while her baby played, or maybe an item of clothing..."

Gabriel wasn't listening anymore. He was concentrating on a new plan.

"We're going to the port," he said.

THE NEW PORT was full of life. It was an area frequented by tourists, as most cargo operations were carried out in the commercial port.

So it was all fried fish and oyster bars and whale-or-shark seeing expeditions during the day, and one of the city party centers at night.

Gabriel stood at the marina and looked at the big yachts parked there. He could see inside some of them. There were framed pictures on the walls and candles and fruit bowls. Some very rich people kept their yachts in the New Port.

"This looks interesting ... and quite apropos," Maurice said, pointing at something down the marina.

"Underwater Safari!" read a merry-colored banner next to a bright yellow submarine, which looked like from a cartoon, even though it could fit maybe twenty or thirty people. Opposite the vessel there was a booth where a smiling woman sold tickets and talked with interested customers.

He stopped by the booth and read the sign.

Wonders of the Underwater World. Take a trip in a real submarine, MON-FRI 12AM-8PM, SAT-SUN 8AM-8PM

Gabriel walked past the booth and approached the submarine.

"Come out," he whispered.

The demon was a young, assertive man in navy clothes.

"Hi there, land rat! I'm Jacques, and this is my submarine! Can I interest you in a marvelous journey under the surface of the ocean, to see the bottom and what strange creatures live there?"

"There are strange creatures?" Gabriel asked with genuine interest.

"Well, fish mostly, but very different from those you can see close to the surface. Also, crabs, mussels, and rusty mechanisms which could very well be wrecks of old ships from who knows how long ago!"

"There are shipwrecks? Really?"

"Hm, I doubt that," admitted Jacques. "That's what my captain tells the tourists. I suspect it mostly some old port machinery, like old sunken cranes, you know?"

"I see."

"Come on, buy the ticket! Aboard, we keep normal atmospheric conditions, so even pregnant women, heart patients, and persons with ear problems are safe and comfortable! We also offer luxury seats and large viewports, allowing you to witness the wonders of the underwater realm firsthand in a panoramic experience like no other."

"Speaking of the underwater realm, have you maybe heard of a submarine on the bottom of the bay?"

"How do you mean...? Neptune-7 tourist submarines like me are the safest model to ever grace the waters..."

"No, no, a real submarine."

"I'm a real submarine."

"A military one. Have you heard rumors of a military submarine stuck on the bottom of Los Maines Bay?"

"Ah ... you know what? Now I think about it, maybe I heard something ... but I didn't pay it much thought, as these days submarines are very safe..."

"I'm sure you're the safest," Gabriel interrupted. "What did you hear?"

"I heard something from the fishing nets of one of the old trawlers. It was *Telemachus'*, I think."

THE FISHING PORT was much quieter. The old fishing trawlers, with chipped paint, smelling of fish and salt, floated in lines at the pier. *Telemachus* was a medium-sized ship painted half-red, half-white. There was nobody around apart from the odd seagull standing on its roof.

The nets lay in the stern, entangled, full of seaweeds and rotting.

"Net, come out," said Gabriel, and a stout, hardened woman appeared on the trawler, wearing a fisherman's hat and a waterproof coat. She had only one tooth.

"Well, I be damned, for the curse of Neptune Poseidon's bitch!" she cried. "What did the currents carry here? A proper hoity-toity Ombudsman to grace this old smelly roll of fisherman's net. What brings me the honor?"

She spat into the water.

"I've heard you saw a submarine on the bottom of our bay," Gabriel said.

"Ain't that the truth, pretty boy. But it was years ago! Glad somebody got interested in it at last. I saw a dark, long shape stuck on the bottom. And maybe my rheumatism is killing my legs, but my eyes are still good, and I know a submarine when I see one, even from that far."

"Where exactly was it?"

"It was a dark and stormy day," the Net said. "The old wind blew like seven on the Beaufort scale. And the old goat of the captain and his good-for-nothing pals of course were drunk out of their minds. That's their style of fishing, you know. And the winds and the waves carried us much farther than usual from our normal fishing ground. They dragged me across half the sea, it felt. And then I saw it, low, low below me. A real damn submarine on the bottom."

"I would need some more specific location..." Gabriel said, and looked at the control panel visible through the window of the bridge. "You have a navigation computer or something? I don't even know how half of those things are called. Let's ask the whole trawler. Come out!"

The demon of the boat was an old, bearded Greek, playing with some *begleri* beads in his hand.

"Yes?" he yelled. "What is it?"

"You don't have to scream, I'm standing next to you," Gabriel grimaced. "You remember the dark and stormy day the Net told me about, when the captain and his pals got drunk out of their minds?"

"Sounds like most of my days, son!" shouted the demon.

"Oh, the day when that stupid goat Luther fell overboard, remember?" said the Net. "Or is your mind already eaten by the scurvy and syphilis!"

"Of course, of course!" the Trawler started laughing. "That was some fun. Well, what can I tell ya? Our grounds are at, like, eight miles west from the Old Port, I'd say, and on that day we drifted, say, around five miles to the North and three miles to the West, I would say?"

"Aye, sounds about right," the Net said.

"Thank you," Gabriel said and turned to Maurice. "Let's go and get some rest back at the hotel. We're going sailing tonight."

24

———

THE SLEEPING DEATH

IT WAS AFTER MIDNIGHT. Gabriel walked along the marina of the New Port. A huge Ferris wheel, lit like a whole carnival, spun behind him. Smells attacked his nostrils: shish kebabs, souvlaki, cobs of corn on a grill, and so-called elephant ears—circles of deep-fried dough sprinkled with powdered sugar. There were still far too many people than he had hoped for, and music played from several bars, but it was enough to take one step away from the promenade to be engulfed in darkness, which only sparse lanterns dispelled with their mortuary-cold bluish light.

Gabriel crouched in the darkness next to the submarine.

"Hey you," he said. "Come out."

"Hi again!" said Jacques. "I see I managed to tempt you with the panoramic experience of an underwater safari! Sadly, I must ask you to come tomorrow, as we're closed..."

"Do you have headlights?" Gabriel interrupted him.

"I have most powerful headlights of five-thousand Lumens, revealing every corner of coral reefs."

"How about oxygen? Won't I suffocate in there?"

"For one person? The aggregators will last at least six hours."

"It's not a lot."

"Our trips usually take only sixty to ninety minutes…"

Gabriel looked towards the brightly lit commercial center, full of drunken cries and noisy music. There was nobody coming.

"I'm asking hypothetically. If you were to go down to the ocean floor … fifteen miles away from here … could you make it you think? Is it too deep or too far?"

"What's there?" Jacques asked suspiciously. "A sunken treasure of some kind?"

"You can call it that."

"Well. I don't think it's beyond my capabilities. Hypothetically. Past the shallows, the ocean around here is around two-thousand feet deep. I'm certified for six hundred and fifty. It's my so-called test depth. The hull should take the pressure. But it would be taking chances … I wouldn't advise it."

"Let's go, then."

"What? You said that was all hypothetical…"

"And now I say let's go for a night adventure," Gabriel winked at the demon.

"No! My owner and captain isn't here! Come in the morning and have a word with him."

"No, we're not waiting for your owner and captain," Gabriel said and made the Sign of the Covenant. "Open up. But be quiet. No lights until we go down."

"Very well. But be advised I warn severely against such careless action, setting out so deep and far away without skilled personnel…"

"Okay, okay … get on it."

The port on the submarine opened.

"Unmoor me," said the demon. "Can't do it on my own."

Gabriel grabbed the thick green rope, secured to a pier cleat.

"No!" hissed the demon. "It stays. Unfasten those on board."

Gabriel heard people approaching and he quickly stepped on the narrow deck of the submarine and hid behind the plastic fin. They were lovers walking side by side, embracing, and their steps were uneven and wavering from alcohol consumption, while an Elvis impersonator belched out his *Viva Las Vegas* from a British "Home away from home" pub, fighting for the upper hand with a football game broadcasting on the TV of a neighboring joint.

When they were finally gone with their kissing and cooing, Gabriel slid into the cabin and closed the port. It was a small room with two rows of seats along the sides. The viewports were made of fortified glass or something similar. In the front, behind another set of doors, was the pilot's cabin.

"Let's go, " Gabriel said.

"This won't end well," Jacques moaned. The vessel trembled as the engine jumped to life and they began backing away from the marina.

Gabriel sat on a plastic chair in darkness and watched through the window as the lights of the port behind grew smaller and smaller.

"We'll be passing the last breakwaters," Jacques said, and pointed to a black opening between two pulsing lights, red and green. "They can spot us there. You need to call the harbor master's office if you travel at night ... and you need to have the proper lightning."

"Go underwater, then," Gabriel said.

"Aye, aye, Ombudsman," the demon said. Gabriel shivered with unease as the submarine descended and black water came higher and higher on the viewports until they got lost in total darkness.

"Turn on the headlights! Can you see anything?" Gabriel cried.

Twin, super bright lamps came on at the front, revealing the bottom of the harbor, strewn with old anchors and waste—bottles, containers, floating parts of old ropes—and two monstrous pillars of the port, made of reinforced concrete, overgrown with undulating moss.

As they passed between them and the bottom quickly subsided and disappeared from view, they were surrounded with dimly lit water, greenish in hue, with medusas or an odd fish swimming by.

It was a totally new experience for Gabriel. He rarely went out to sea. The last time he remembered was a short whale watching trip with school, on which no whales were observed, as opposed to many examples of seasickness—probably caused by a few forbidden beverages smuggled onto the boat by the students. This was different. This was like a trip into the bowels of Mother Earth. The ever-present hum, which was maybe the engine, maybe the water pressing on the hull, made him feel claustrophobic. Thousands of cubic meters of water pressed on them from each direction. He felt panic and fought the urge to order the demon to take them to the surface immediately, but the thought of giving Matt his long-lost father prevailed. He killed his mother. Finding his father was the least he could do. He owed him that.

The chances were so slim. Who could survive underwater for so long? Maurice had mentioned the nuclear air aggregates and pounds of rations, but even if that was true, what were they doing for so long in those depths? What spy mission could take them that long?

Gabriel took a deep breath to calm himself. He searched for Maurice, but the demon hid himself in his wristband. He never liked water.

An hour passed, and the surrounding ocean got darker and they could see no bottom anymore. They slowed down.

"We should be around there," Jacques said. "Eleven miles

west from the Old Port, five miles north. What were we supposed to find here? Because I see nothing."

"Go deeper," Gabriel said.

The demon sighed and Gabriel heard another sound as the propellers pushed them down. It was getting darker. He could hear some cracking.

"We can't go any deeper!" cried the demon. "The pressure is getting too much for me. The hull may break."

"Go deeper!" cried Gabriel, looking around through the viewports. Far below them, faintly lit by their headlights, they could see the ocean bottom, like the surface of the Moon.

"Goddamnit!" yelled Jacques, and a long crack appeared in the window. The sound of the engine changed its pitch, became higher, almost plaintive. "Do you ever want to see the light of day again, boy? We need to surface."

"There!" cried Gabriel and pointed. Ahead of them and below, a long, majestic form hung in the water, stuck on the ocean floor, completely dark and immobile.

"What is it, for the beard of Neptune?" Jacques asked.

"It's a Russian submarine where my father is a spy," Gabriel replied with his voice breaking from emotion. "Go there. Go closer."

"Ombudsman," hissed the demon. "We will die. We are cracking under pressure! I'm not made for such depths!"

"Listen to me!" yelled Gabriel, making the Sign again. The chances were so slim, but if their father were really trapped there, that would mean the end of all troubles, that would mean happiness without borders for the two brothers lost in the dark, incomprehensible world.

They went closer. The shape was soon revealed to be indeed a long submarine, quiet and dark.

The glass in their window cracked some more and water slowly began dripping to the floor. Something howled and cracked in the back, and the submarine tilted to one side.

"We lost one engine!" Jacques cried in panic.

"Move closer!" Gabriel yelled.

They moved to within thirty feet from the submarine. Gabriel could see the letters in Cyrillic painted on its side, the disabled engines, and the dark tower on the top.

"There!" he said and pointed. Next to the submarine, a woman in a foreign-looking uniform was floating in the water, her hair swimming around her face from under a forage cap with a Russian emblem. Her eyes were closed but she wasn't dead; her chest rose and fell.

"Is she dead? Who is she?" Gabriel asked.

"She's asleep. It's the demon of the submarine," Jacques replied. "We need to go up. Ten seconds more and we're dead!"

"Hey you!" Gabriel cried and made the Sign of the Covenant. "Wake up!"

The woman opened her eyes and stared straight at him. Then she disappeared and red and green lights appeared on the Russian submarine's sides, the water swirled behind its tail, and clouds of sand arose around the black giant as it lifted from the bottom.

"Ombudsman! We're breaking!" Jacques shouted in panic. "We will die here!"

"Where are you going?" shouted Gabriel to the Russian submarine, but it didn't listen, or maybe it didn't hear him through the water.

He watched in horror as the window of his submarine cracked, and a stream of water filled the cabin.

"Go up!" he cried to Jacques. "Fast as you can!"

Water burst into the cabin in streams from four sides as the engine roared and howled, pushing them towards the surface. The water got into electronics; there was a plume of sparks and the lights went off. In total darkness, Gabriel felt the water rising to his chest. He started to swim, but he soon felt the roof above his head, and he could just tilt his neck to gasp for air in the darkness.

Water started to spill into his open mouth and into his nostrils. He caught one last breath. The last thing he heard was Jacques' cry: "I'm dying!"

Gabriel flailed around in the darkness, trying to find the way out of the submarine, which had become his trap.

25

—————

AS THE WORLD ENDS

He got to what felt like the viewport and banged it with his elbow, trying to smash it. His lungs burned. A paroxysm of pain twisted his body, and at the same time he felt his consciousness drifting away—he was a tiny star of being in an endless dark space, no sex, no name, no history, and no body. He understood it was the end.

Then some force bent his body and he drew air through the nose and instantly began vomiting water and coughed, lying on the floor of the cabin. He opened his eyes and saw it was night. Jacques had made it to the surface. Gabriel felt a wave of bitter disappointment; his struggle wasn't over yet, the muscles couldn't rest; life was violence and toil. Then, he remembered what he had been doing up to this point.

He sat on the floor and looked through the broken viewport.

He saw Maurice standing outside, on the front of their small submarine, staring ahead without a word.

Gabriel got to his feet, and coughing up the salty ocean water which burned his nostrils, he opened the hatch and went to the deck to join the demon.

"Maurice?" he said. "What are you doing?"

But the demon didn't answer. He kept staring ahead, and

when Gabriel followed his stare, he could only see the calm waves reflecting the light of stars.

And then it happened. With a terrible roar, and an explosion of foam, a blunt-nosed rocket dashed up from underwater, hung in the air briefly, then a blinding flame erupted from its tail, with billows of smoke. The heatwave hit Gabriel, and he shut his eyes, covered his face, and dropped down to the deck. As he felt the heat recede a little, with his skin still burning from the scalding heat, he lifted his head to look.

The ballistic missile, carried by the roaring flame, rose up the sky. Its trajectory tilted and it flew towards the land behind them.

"Maurice? What is going on?" he asked the demon, who followed the rocket with his lava-like, yellow eyes.

"It is done," Maurice said, and disappeared.

"What? Maurice! Come out!" Gabriel cried and shook his wristband, but with no effect.

He heard a distant hum of engines, and where the missile got off, in the distance he saw the Russian submarine come to the surface, its majestic, oblong hull streaming water from its ducts, and it stayed there, immobile and sinister.

He looked around, feeling lost and clueless. Even Maurice was gone. Something very bad was happening and he couldn't understand. But nothing good could come from staying on the broken vessel.

He jumped in the water and swam towards the Russian submarine.

The water was cold, and the submarine was much farther away than he thought. With panic, he understood he couldn't make it; his arms were going numb. He raised his hand in the Sign of the Covenant and cried out, hoping the sub would hear him:

"Submarine! Come closer!"

It took a second of sinking hope as he stared at the immobile colossus, but then its engines turned on and it slowly moved towards him. He looked at the tall, majestic vessel when a woman's voice said in a Russian accent:

"There's a ladder on the starboard, comrade Ombudsman."

He grabbed the slimy rung and just rested for a while, catching his breath. Then he climbed the metal ladder up to the dorsal of the submarine. The topside deck had several circular domes on both sides. One of them was open, revealing a deep tube. Smoke rose from the opening.

He saw the demon of the submarine, the woman in the forage cap he'd woken up, floating above the fin. He approached her.

"What was that?" he shouted, pointing to the horizon where the rocket had disappeared.

The demon looked at him with her steely calm eyes.

"An Azyar-6 ballistic missile, carrying nuclear warheads. Target: Washington, DC. Estimated time of impact: eighteen minutes."

"What?" he cried. "What have you done?"

"I did my duty. I did what my captain ordered me to do before the saboteur disabled all systems. I started a nuclear war."

"What?" Gabriel repeated, laughing with disbelief that was turning into horror.

"The American nuclear response systems must have initiated the retaliatory strike already. To which Russia will answer. In half an hour, the sky above will swarm with intercontinental ballistic missiles. In two hours, the Earth will turn into a furnace. These are the last moments of life on this planet, comrade Ombudsman."

"Why did you do that?"

"I told you. My captain, Vitaliy Ivanovich Promenkov, commanded it. I had watched him lie sleeplessly for many nights before, muttering to himself about the need to punish the

Evil Empire of the United States of America. He feigned the order from the high command at the Kremlin. He gave the commands, the crew programmed the target coordinates, and engaged the launch procedure. At the last moment, the saboteur got into the power room and disabled all systems. Darkness filled me and I fell asleep. You woke me up. So I fulfilled my duty."

Gabriel sat on the metal deck and hid his face in his hands.

He sat like that for some minutes, waiting for the end of it all, but then remembered the last thing he could do before that happened.

"Submarine..." he said, finally.

"My name is Typhoon, comrade Ombudsman," the demon answered.

"Has anyone of your crew ... survived?'

The submarine laughed with sadness in her voice.

"The saboteur barricaded himself in the power room and cut off the reactor, including the air aggregators, thus sacrificing his life to save the world. No human can survive without air, and it has been five years. Only ghosts roam my corridors."

"My father was among your crew."

"Really? What was his name?"

"Michael West ... but he must've been under a different name. He was a spy."

"A spy among submariners, all of them trained since youth in Severomorsk, who spent their lives at Russian navy bases?" Typhoon laughed again and shook her head. "I find it highly improbable."

"Let me in," Gabriel said.

Typhoon just pointed at a nearby hatch.

He pulled it open. A terrible stench wafted from the inside, something stale and long rotten. Gabriel waited for a moment to fight the nausea, moved his head away to take a deep breath of fresh air, and descended the ladder.

The inside of the submarine was mostly metal: metal walls, metal floor, tubes and wires on the sides and above. Everything hummed and vibrated slightly. It was cramped and lit with lamps in wire cages. It was unpleasant to spend a minute here, let alone a month or more as submariners were wont to do.

He saw the first corpse at the foot of the ladder. The mummified face with no lips bared its yellow teeth at him in a grimace of agony. The corpse was dressed in a blue uniform with a white wide collar, and had a name tag Gabriel couldn't read, as it was in Cyrillic.

"Senior Seaman Golyatsov," said Typhoon coldly.

In the last minutes of life on Earth, Gabriel pushed himself through the claustrophobic corridors of the Russian submarine, looking at the corpses of the mariners, some of them curled on the floor, some embracing, while some met their suffocating fate at their workstations, their heads resting on keyboards and control panels. The demon of the submarine recited their names. They were dead, buried in their underwater tomb for long years, until he'd disturbed their resting place, a strange museum of an underwater war machine.

He got to a power room and tried to open the entrance hatch.

"It's locked from the other side," Typhoon said.

"Open up!" Gabriel made the Sign.

The hatch opened and he stepped into the power room filled with more control panels and screens. A man lay on his face, a pistol in his dark, rotten hand. Gabriel reached out and turned the man over onto his back. The dry, mummified face was disfigured, but he was sure he didn't recognize it. The man was shorter and stouter than his father.

"Anatoliy Sozhnetsov," said the Submarine. "The saboteur."

There was a piece of paper next to him, a note, written in longhand.

"What does it say?" Gabriel asked.

Typhoon read aloud: "Tatyana, Pola, Misha, my little lion, I love you more than anything in the world, A.S."

Gabriel nodded. He stood there for a while, resigned, then turned back and went to the exit. He climbed the ladder to the surface. He breathed fresh night air with relief, even though the knowledge of the incoming apocalypse lay heavy on his chest.

"Missiles, come out!" he snapped.

There were eleven of them, with long pointy bald heads, smiling wide with their monstrous mouths full of sharp pointy teeth like piranhas.

He clenched his jaw, took out the Kanchak from a calf pocket in his cargo pants, and stabbed each of the demons. They died one after another with terrible high-pitched shrieks, and the domes under which the missiles were housed turned into black pumice stone.

Having killed all the missiles, he sat on a hatch and stared to the horizon, toward land, and waited for the all-consuming fire.

He thought about what he was leaving behind. It wasn't much. He hadn't had a very happy life. He thought about Matt. He should be asleep now. Better that way, to just go from sleep into death. Unless the city sirens woke him to the terror of the nuclear holocaust.

He thought about Andrea, the girl who had told him he would cause the end of the world.

"Typhoon?" he said.

"Yes, comrade Ombudsman?"

"Set course for Omelsen Rock. Full ahead," he said.

He stood on the deck as the submarine broke the waves, moving through the ocean towards the land, looming in the distance.

26

———

FIRE

THE SUBMARINE STOPPED a hundred feet away from the land.

"It is too shallow for me to continue," Typhoon told Gabriel.

Gabriel jumped off the deck into the water and swam towards the rock ahead.

Soon he felt the bottom under his feet and he walked up, soaking wet, to the rocky wall. Omelsen Rock rose above him.

"Andrea!" he cried, but nobody answered.

He walked around the rock to where the shore was least steep. He climbed it.

He walked up the path that led to the top of Omelsen Rock and saw the smoke rising up from the hill.

On the grassy cliff, smashing the trees, there lay the huge missile. Smoke rose from its snout.

Gabriel looked around.

Andrea lay on the rock, not giving signs of life. He ran up to her and lifted her head.

"Andrea," he whispered. He felt a pulse in her neck and saw she was breathing. There was some dried blood under her nose.

"Resting, I suppose. After spoiling everything," said a familiar voice behind him.

Gabriel turned around and saw Maurice crouching next to

the fallen, mangled rocket, touching it with his palm and stroking it like it was a sick, dying person. There was a small fire in the grass next to him.

"I warned you against her," Maurice continued. "That's women for you."

Gabriel put Andrea's head back on the ground, stood up and turned to Maurice.

"What happened here?" he asked sharply.

The demon of the playground looked at him calmly from under the brim of his old vagabond hat.

"Well ... the missile was going up, minding its own business. But your friend here had to interfere. She screamed her lungs off, like a banshee or something, and extinguished the power and all systems. The poor baby fell from the sky ... and I'm afraid it's useless now. As for your friend, I guess she is exhausted or something."

Gabriel crouched for a second to take the Kanchak knife from his pocket. The demon looked at the blade without much interest.

"Maurice," Gabriel said. "Who are you?"

"I'm your friend," the demon said. "A friendly former demon of a city playground, currently a demon of one boy's leather wristband ... who saved the aforementioned boy's life multiple times."

"You gave me the dreams about my father. You lied about what Crowe's phone told you, about the submarine. My father hadn't even set foot in it. "

"Everybody makes mistakes."

"No. You knew about the missile..." Gabriel's voice was breaking from emotion. "You wanted to use me to destroy the world. Why?"

Something about these words made Maurice's face change. It grew more serious and darker. He stood up to his whole six-feet five-inches height, staring down at Gabriel.

"Out of love, what else?" he answered. "The things we do for love."

"Love?"

"I'm in love with him." Maurice smiled gently and pointed with his head to the eastern horizon, where above the gray line of the ocean a tiny speck of gold appeared, the first sliver of the rising sun. The eyes with which Maurice looked at the sun were so similar to it— creeping, flaming lava. "From the first sight. Since the day I was born."

"You wanted to destroy the Earth because you love the sun?" Gabriel laughed with incredulity. "Stop fucking with me."

"Not destroy. Burn the Earth. It's a subtle difference, no? How can I ever hope to get his attention otherwise? This divine, life-giving, cosmic sphere of pure flame, gigantic... You people are so pathetic these days. You see things every day and never pay it any attention. But eons ago you knew a god when you saw it. Today it's just sunglasses, suntan lotion, and air conditioning."

"You wanted to burn the Earth to show off to the sun, to make it notice you?"

Maurice bared his clenched teeth. "I wanted the world to explode in an orgasm, in a union with the sun, yes, boy, small boy. What can you know about these things? In 1955, at the explosion of Tsar Bomba, the most powerful device ever deployed in human history, fifty megatons, shattering glass in windows seven hundred kilometers away, its blast wave circling the globe three times, that's when I got a glitter of hope in my eternal longing. I wandered the Earth and looked for a chance. And I found it. I learned about the missing nuclear submarine, its captain and the saboteur. So I used you! What do you know? You, whom I led by the hand through the burning prison unscathed."

Gabriel stared at Maurice with an open mouth. He felt betrayal so crushing he couldn't believe it.

"Ricko Boleani knew you," he said. "He looked at you before

killing himself. You said he didn't, but he did. You had tried to use him before me. That's why you knew him so well."

"There's only so many Ombudsmen in the world. One can't be picky," Maurice replied. "And you all have this sad affliction, this tumor or whatever it's called in your brain, that makes you able to see us. It has this sad quality to grow and change you into murderous psychopaths, caring only about your sadistic impulses. Ricko's tumor was sadly very advanced, and he soon chose his strange pleasures over listening to my sage advice."

"So you decided to kill him, with my hands."

"You can't be sorry for him."

"Wait ... wait..." Gabriel felt a tingling in his hands and feet. Blood rushed from his head and he felt as if he were about to faint. "You led him to Matt ... because I didn't want to accept your offer. You made him kidnap Matt. It's all because of you." He felt a trace of water slide down his cheek and realized he was crying.

"Look at it this way," Maurice replied calmly. "Because of some short, although indeed and indisputably unpleasant time your brother spent in his basement, we managed to save the remaining children from death and torture ... and who knows how many more when you think about his future victims. I told you we were going to do great things together. Pity the greatest one didn't go so well."

Gabriel lowered his head. He couldn't think straight. He was paralyzed with this newfound knowledge. His mind was in chaos.

"I agree it all could've gone better," Maurice admitted. "But you are sad? Look at me. I just lost my thousand-year-old dream. And I'm left with even more years of solitude and the impossible, painful hunger."

Gabriel lifted his face. Tears stung his skin, scalded by the missile's exhaust. He clenched his hand on the Kanchak knife.

"Your sick little plan led to me killing my mother!" he cried in a breaking voice. He rushed at Maurice and stabbed him in the heart with the Prince's demon-killing dagger.

The blade went through Maurice's chest as if it were made of air.

They stood there for a second, staring in each other's eyes, and suddenly the whole of Maurice's body stood in flames, his head, his arms, his torso, burning bright. Gabriel jumped back, tripped and fell. He looked at the burning demon standing before him, smiling at him. The knife didn't kill him.

"Who are you?" Gabriel whispered in awe.

"I am Fire."

Gabriel stared at Maurice's face made of flames and so many things became clear—his hate of water, his ability to make Gabriel resistant to heat, his lava-like eyes, different from other demons...

"You understand now?" Maurice asked in a gentle voice. "I'm not a demon. I am Fire. You're talking about showing off to the sun. No! I'd match it, swallowing the whole planet. A mighty, great sphere of flame in the cosmos. Another sun. Little boy, there are great forces at play in the world. And you are only a little boy."

"I will kill you one day," Gabriel replied.

Maurice stared at him for some more time with a smile of sympathy.

"Unlike my snobbish cousins, I have always liked working with people," he said. "You're unbelievable."

"I will kill you," Gabriel repeated.

"Good luck killing an element, boy."

Maurice tipped his hat, turned his back to Gabriel, patted the missile one more time, walked away into the air and disappeared.

Gabriel felt a tingling on his hand and looked. His leather wristband turned to ash. A gust of wind blew it apart and set the particles of ash dancing in the air.

· · ·

GABRIEL PICKED UP ANDREA. She was lighter than he thought. He could see how thin she had become.

Step by step, carrying her in his arms, he walked away from the fallen missile and Omelsen Rock, through the forest, towards the nearest road.

The forest road was empty. The sun was getting higher above the trees and warmed his bones—the heat coming from millions of miles away.

"Li," Gabriel said, carrying Andrea down the road. "You with me?"

"I am waterproof, IP rating 68, unlike some expensive models by a company I'm not going to name," came Li's calm answer from his pocket. "How can I help you, Ombudsman?"

"Call an ambulance," he said. "Tell them where we are. And, Li…?"

"Yes, Ombudsman?"

"Call me Gabriel."

"Sure, Omb—Gabriel! And how about Gabe?"

"That would be fine, Li. That would be fine."

The long road led straight through the forest towards the city. He could see the gray skyline of Los Maines shimmering in the morning haze. Above the skyscrapers, the giant goddess-like face of Los Maines' spirit looked in his direction as he walked down the forest road carrying the unconscious girl.

ANDREA STRETCHED AND YAWNED. She felt so good. She felt the honey-like happiness of a sweet slumber you never want to end. She opened her eyes and saw she was tiny in the flower again, lying on the bed of carpels. She could hear that most beautiful song very, very, softly in the unfathomable distance, on the verge of hearing.

"You did well, Eden." She recognized the Horned One's voice booming softly above her home flower. "Your watch is over. You saw the Rising Star rise above the waters and you extinguished its flame."

Andrea smiled as she felt a wave of pleasure crawl up from her feet, along her legs, and spill all over her body. She shivered.

"It feels good," she said dreamily.

"Rest now after all the hardship and pain," the Horned One said. "It will be a night of song, and dance, and love."

"Yes," she said.

"Rest and take pleasure in this secret meadow, because soon you have to return to the place you're from, Eden. And carry on with your task of extinguishing the lights. Humans have to return to their caves and forests. Cities have to grow quiet and covered with fresh grass as you reclaim the eternal order. As you bring the darkness back to the night."

EPILOGUE

GABRIEL STOPPED his bike at the rehab center's garden. The garden was large and lush, with patients walking slowly on its paths like phantoms, or sitting on the benches. He locked his bike in a rack.

"Thank you for the new tires, Gabriel!" cried a happy Giovanni. "They're even better than the old ones. Smooth and firm, just how I like them!"

"Sure, Giovanni," Gabriel answered and smiled.

He went down the alley between chestnut trees, passing a marble sign that read: "Sunny Meadows Center."

Agent Delancey sat in the lobby behind a table full of self-help books about fighting addiction. He looked like death, in a t-shirt that was too big on him, his hair disheveled, shadows under his protruding cheekbones, his eyes staring darkly under his scarred forehead.

"Hi, Agent," Gabriel said, looking at the books put out on Delancey's table, the colorful covers with laughing families, flowers, and doves.

"Nobody buys the fucking things," Delancey said glumly.

Gabriel sat on a chair on the opposite end of the table.

"How are you doing, Agent?"

"How do you think I'm doing? I'm miserable, like all the poor damn sons-of-bitches here."

"You started a publishing business?" Gabriel joked, gesturing at the self-help brochures.

"That's part of the whole rehab therapy supposedly. Turning me into a well-functioning part of society, learning to do honest work. Beats hoeing our carrot field, as far as I'm concerned."

Gabriel laughed.

"And how are you doing, son? Your brother?"

"He's doing fine at the house. He's talking a bit more. I saw him today, from the outside. Seems he has a friend. And me, well, I'm getting the second dose of those rabies shots later today."

"And CAISA?"

"Still there. Set up posts in some apartments near the orphanage, too. They thought I wouldn't notice."

Delancey nodded.

"Look out for that Crowe. He can still mess things up for you. He's a clever little jerk."

"He's taller than you, Agent."

"Yeah, don't be a smartass. Most people are taller than me. I was speaking metaphorically. And ... Bea called me. They're investigating those two Princes, as you called them. We still don't know who sent them ... and if there could be more. So ... I guess, you be careful out there, yeah?"

Gabriel nodded.

"I'll be very careful from now on. I've been betrayed badly."

Delancey frowned and lowered his eyes.

"I'm sorry. That's all I will say."

"I don't mean by you. You didn't betray me. You thought you were helping."

"Someone else, then?"

Gabriel nodded again.

"It sucks. Sucky feeling. But, you know, they give us a whole litany of mottoes down here, supposed to help us. One of them I like was 'This, too, will pass.' You know? That bad sucky feeling? That, too, will pass."

Gabriel smiled in response.

"Hey, at least we have each other, right? A junkie and a homeless delinquent," Delancey said with a crooked smile.

"I will buy a book from you," Gabriel said.

"Really?" The agent seemed honestly happy.

"This one," Gabriel pointed at a book with the kitschiest cover, entitled *Life Is Worth Living*.

Delancey handed him the book. "Here you are. It will be four-ninety-nine."

"I'll pay with a card, please."

"Sure thing."

Delancey reached for a card terminal, punched in the amount, which took him some time, trial and error, and handed it to Gabriel.

"It's paid," Gabriel said, and made the Sign of the Covenant.

The terminal buzzed, flashed a "Payment Accepted" message, and printed out the receipt.

Delancey stared glumly as Gabriel took the book, winked at him, and walked towards the exit.

"Smartass," he murmured. "Get out of my shop before I lose my temper."

Outside the therapy center's building, Gabriel squinted in the bright sunlight as he walked towards his bicycle, thinking about the long-haired demon in the shabby hat, covered in flames, who'd been dreaming about the cosmic sphere of fire, longing to burn the world. It was a bad thought, so he shook it off, got on his bike and pedaled back home, to the port city of Los Maines, and his brother, and his girl.

THE END OF BOOK 2

STAY IN TOUCH!

Thank you for reading The Girl Who Brought Darkness.

Don't miss out on new content and join my newsletter! You will be the first to know when I have created something, a book or a game you might enjoy.

You will also get a **free ebook** with four short stories: go to the website www.blazejdzikowski.com

And please also leave a rating or review at Amazon store. You might not believe it, but even a line or two could makes a difference for me and my books!

See you soon ... somewhere in the Hidden Empires.

Blazej

Made in the USA
Middletown, DE
18 March 2022